A powerful and sensitive novel by

NORMA FOX MAZER

Author of

TAKING TERRI MUELLER
MWA Edgar Award
California Young Readers Medal

DOWNTOWN
ALA BEST BOOK FOR YOUNG ADULTS

AFTER THE RAIN

"Beautifully and sensitively written, sounding the basic chords of the pleasures and pains of family relationships. What distinguishes this book, making it linger in the heart, are the realistic portrayals of the tensions, guilt, and sudden, painfully moving moments . . . "

Kirkus Featured Review

"A beautifully moving, heartfelt story"
Publishers Weekly

Avon Books are available at special quantity discounts for bulk purchases for sales promotions, premiums, fund raising or educational use. Special books, or book excerpts, can also be created to fit specific needs.

For details write or telephone the office of the Director of Special Markets, Avon Books, Inc., Dept. FP, 1350 Avenue of the Americas, New York, New York 10019, 1-800-238-0658.

Norma Fox Mazer

After the Rain

AN AVON ⬥ FLARE BOOK

AVON BOOKS, INC.
1350 Avenue of the Americas
New York, New York 10019

Copyright © 1987 by Norma Fox Mazer
Published by arrangement with the author
Library of Congress Catalog Card Number: 86-33270
ISBN: 0-380-75025-2
www.avonbooks.com

First Avon Flare Printing: November 1987

AVON FLARE TRADEMARK REG. U.S. PAT. OFF. AND IN OTHER COUNTRIES, MARCA REGISTRADA, HECHO EN U.S.A.

Printed in the U.S.A

OPM   40   39   38   37   36   35   34   33

For my agents,
Elaine Markson and Geri Thoma,
for their love and support.

ONE

"Look down on this scene," Rachel writes in her notebook. "Three people in a kitchen, sitting around a table. A man, a woman, and a girl." She glances up, squints at her parents. "The three people are together but not together. The man and the woman know the girl is there, but they don't really see her. They see her, but they don't really know her."

Rachel chews on her pen. Should she name them? No, it pleases her to call them "the man," "the woman," and "the girl."

"The kitchen is long and narrow. Cupboard doors stand open, a mop leans against a wall, the calendar is still turned to"—she looks at the calendar over the wall phone—"August, although it's now late September."

Okay, okay, not bad. What next? She studies the linoleum floor. Her mother is a bear about floor washing. Should she put in that the floor is clean? Ho-hum. "The floor," she writes, after a moment, "is fiercely clean. The toaster oven gleams and glows from a recent polishing."

Should she write more for the opening? Or is that already too much? How do you know when to stop? She is working on a story about her family. She hopes it will be a story. So far, in almost two years of dedicated writing—something in the journal every

1

day—she has managed only to write opening sentences, first paragraphs, the beginnings of stories. But even if she finished them, would they be real stories? Aren't stories supposed to come out of your imagination? How will she ever become a writer if the only things she can think to write about are her mother, her father, herself?

Two years ago the writer Wilda Sycora came to their school and talked to Rachel's class in the library. Rachel had read all of Wilda Sycora's books and made sure to get a seat close to the front of the room.

"You don't know how much you have inside you," Wilda Sycora said. "I know there's somebody in this room who wants to be a writer." She pushed her glasses up on her nose, looked around the room. "Whoever you are, don't be afraid of what's inside you. Don't be afraid to invent, to be original, to be yourself."

Sitting hunched over, her arms around herself, Rachel knew those words were meant for her. A space seemed to open in her mind, light poured in, a clear white light, and for a moment she stood in the center of that light.

Now she reads over what she wrote. No. No good. *These* words are meant for the wastebasket. She crosses out everything she's written, then tears the page out of her notebook and rips it into little scraps.

Her mother looks across the table. "Oh, Rachey, your beautiful writing. Was it something for English class?"

Rachel keeps a shielding arm poised over the top of her notebook. Her parents are having their after-supper cup of coffee. The three of them are elbow-to-elbow. How cozy that sounds, like a regular little

Cosby family. Every Thursday night Rachel watches *The Cosby Show* with amazement in her heart. Look at that smart, beautiful mommy! Look at that wise, funny daddy! Look at those gorgeous sisters and cute hunk of a brother, all of them saying clever, funny things to each other faster than anyone can say, "Call a family conference!"

Rachel's family has never had anything remotely like a family conference. They hardly ever say witty things to each other, and nobody is a lawyer or a doctor. Her mother is a secretary; her father runs a little accounting business; her oldest brother, Phil, is a car salesman; and her other brother, Jeremy, is presently a waiter.

She flips to another page in her notebook. She has an English theme to write, which she's been resisting for days, out of sheer boredom. How is it possible that in tenth grade they are still being asked to write "How I Spent My Summer"?

Maybe she ought to write a letter to Mr. Esparza, he of the dark eyes and white linen suits.

Dear Mr. Esparza,
    Sir!
    Mercy on us, your helpless English students. Could you not find it in your heart to assign something better for us to write about than how we spent our summers? As you have been known to say, "a more enlivening topic"? This is a plea from the heart. I fear that one day soon you will walk into English 10 and find nothing but a heap of bored corpses drooped over their notebooks.

Yawningly yours,
Rachel Cooper (Remember me? I'm the one who sits in the third seat in the first row.)

How I Spent My Summer
by Rachel Cooper

My summer was busy and bla bla bla. I was fortunate and bla bla bla to be able to work in my father's office. As my parents both work and I am too old for camp, I was bla bla bla that I would be bored this summer, but that wasn't the bla bla bla bla bla.

How I Spent My Summer
by Rachel Cooper

In brief, my summer was much like other summers—long, hot, and basically uninteresting. I worked a few hours every week in my father's office, filing papers and sweeping the floor. I swam in the high school pool, wrote letters to my brother, and cooked many meals for my parents, all of which were overly appreciated. Overly appreciated, you say? Yes, I say. My parents are lavishly appreciative of any little thing I do. This might sound wonderfully satisfying, but in fact it's embarrassing and even slightly infuriating. It's so patronizing. I often have the feeling that what they praise so highly in me is only their own startled realization that their daughter is an actual, living, breathing person and not a creature who has dropped into their lives from outer . . .

She can't write this theme. It's impossible to be original or inventive. Besides, she knows how she spent her summer; what's on her mind is how she will make it through the rest of her life. How she will ever become something other than what she is now.

"What am I going to do with my life?" she says into the air.

Her father, having just forked in a large piece of chocolate cake, mumbles through the crumbs and points to his mouth. Sometimes Rachel thinks he looks like a Buddha: the rounded, fat shoulders; the little, fat breasts; the puffy cheeks. Other times he appears to her as a baby whale. A baby whale in a yellow sport shirt, voluminous checked pants.

He wipes his rosebud mouth. "Your whole life is a big subject, sweetheart. Don't worry about it. One thing at a time, Mouse. Things will work out for you, you'll see."

Rachel ignores that he called her Mouse, waits for more wisdom, but that's it. One thing at a time. As a wise saying it rates—maybe—a four. Too bad. Rachel feels the need for wisdom. She's fifteen, that's not being a kid anymore, and it frightens her how much she doesn't know. What's life all about, anyway? Oh, okay, you go to college, you get your degree, you find a job—and after that, what? You get married? Do the same thing day after day? Worry about money? And supposing you don't get married, then what? What do you do besides work?

And all that aside, there are other things that are pretty frightening in the world. Why do so many people everywhere, every day, get hurt in so many terrible ways? Why is there a song called "After-the-Bomb Blues"? Why can't she be sure she'll grow up before the world blows up? And even if she does make it, does she want to? Does she want to be old?

Don't worry about it? She can't help worrying. She worries about lots of things. Big things, like The Future. And smaller things like her looks. Her lack of a social life. She doesn't regard it as admirable

5

that this stuff worries her almost as much as the nuclear bomb, but the truth is, she probably puts in more actual worry time on her looks than on the bomb. In the middle of the night she's capable of waking up and going full speed ahead on truly small-potatoes worrying: *What will I wear to school tomorrow? Oh, God! The backs of my arms are like alligator skin. Why did Jeff What's-his-face walk by me in the hall without even a nod?* Maybe she has to worry about something. Maybe it's in her genes, worry genes, of which she must have received a full dose from each parent.

Concentrate, Rachel tells herself, looking down at her notebook. Do not think. Write this theme. Her parents are talking, but that's not the trouble. She often does her homework to the background music of their voices. Background music—how sweet that sounds, as in violins and cellos.

"They took blood from my father," her mother is saying in a high, worried voice. "Manny, you should have seen his arm." Shirley's voice cracks on certain notes, and she appears to go breathless as she speaks.

"Blood?" Rachel's father says in a rumbly, wheezy, but equally anxious voice. "They took blood from Izzy because he had a bellyache? What sense does that make?"

"Well, his age," Shirley says breathlessly. "I suppose the doctor wants to be extra careful."

Rachel studies her mother. Shirley is wearing her at-home clothes: baggy, faded blue sweatshirt, rumpled denim jeans. Her behind is enormous, her legs long and thin. She gets up, clatters the cups into the sink, runs the water hard. "They must have jabbed Daddy in twelve places." She snorts through her long, thin nostrils, and Rachel thinks that if her fa-

6

ther is in the whale family, then her mother must be in the moose family.

As for herself—that's easy. Moose and whale produce mouse.

Mouse. The awful family nickname. Her father stuck it on her at birth. She has heard the story innumerable times. How no one knew her mother was pregnant, including her mother. "My age, who thought about being pregnant at forty-six? My baby days were over. So I thought. But somebody else thought otherwise." A flirtatious little look at Rachel's father. "And then I'm heavyset and my weight goes up and down all the time, so I thought I was gaining a little weight. Until you began kicking inside me. Was I surprised!"

At which point Rachel's father always says, "And then, when you were born, Rachey, this little, tiny, hairless, pink thing, I said to your mother, 'No wonder you didn't know, Shirley! Look at this mouse you've been carrying around inside you!'"

Rachel dreams of delivering an ultimatum. Shirley. Manny. Parents! From this moment on, you will stop calling me Mouse. They will look at her open-mouthed, confused. *Either I'm a mouse or I'm a human being.* Applause, applause. These words will go down in history. Schoolchildren will study them. Books of quotations will always include them. Everyone, everywhere, will know these famous, stirring words—everyone except Shirley and Manny.

Because Rachel will never say it, not that way. She cannot bring herself to tell her parents straight out how she feels. She thinks about telling them, all right. But how she thinks about it is as something very hard to do. Exceptionally difficult. Impossible.

Her friend Helena doesn't agree. "You want to tell them, Rachel, just do it. Just tell them." That's okay for Helena. Life holds no unnecessary complications for her. Besides, she can say things like that and not upset people. Helena's got charm to spare.

Do a Helena, Rachel tells herself. Don't worry about things in advance. Try to be charming and cute. *Maybe you haven't noticed, folks, but I'm not a mouse, folks.*

But she's not a rat, either, and easy as it might seem to Helena to tell her parents any little thing, Rachel knows the moose and the whale are different.

They are old. They are as old as Helena's grandparents. Older, actually. They are grandparents themselves. And they are sensitive. Her father cries easily when hurt by one of his children. Her mother's face takes on a bluish tinge. They only have to talk about Rachel's brother Jeremy, for instance—Jeremy with his spectacular ability to louse up his marriages and his jobs—and there's Manny, leaking tears like a faulty faucet and Shirley, so blue that she seems in immediate need of mouth-to-mouth resuscitation. No, Rachel isn't about to tell them to stop calling her their pet, private name for her. They are old and full of troubles, and she is young and strong and has the oppressive power to hurt their feelings.

And just then, as if to demonstrate the truth of her thoughts, her father turns to her with a sweet expression. "So, Mouse, how's the homework coming?"

You call me Mouse? Again? Gimme Rat! Gimme Wolf! Gimme anything but Mouse. "It's okay," Rachel says.

"You're going to be on the honor roll again, sweetheart?"

She nods.

8

And now her mother turns to her, too. "Are you going to wash your hair tonight?"

"Why do you bother her?" her father says. "If she wants to wash her hair, she'll wash her hair. She doesn't need you to remind her."

Shirley passes her hand over Rachel's head. "Her hair looks so pretty when it's clean. Pretty and shining." She leans toward Rachel, chin in hand. "You're pretty, Rachey, you remind me of my cousin. The same wonderful smile. Manny, doesn't she remind you of my cousin Estelle?"

"Mouse is prettier."

"Estelle was so pretty."

"Did I say she wasn't? I only said Mouse is prettier. Look at her. Look at that pretty child."

They beam on her.

TWO

Dear Brother Jeremy,

I'm feeling sad about myself. I think I have a mean streak. I know I have a bad temper. It doesn't show itself all the time, so I go along and I forget it, and then—I blow up. I just did it. I just blew up at Ma over nothing. Only, when it was happening, I didn't know it was nothing. I was all caught up in it. I wasn't thinking, just blowing up, exploding, going nuts. Has this ever happened to you? It's like the cyclone in *The Wiz*—*whoooosh!* it hits you and you're swept up and you've got nothing to say about it.

Wanna know what happened? We're in the kitchen—Ma, Dad, and me. They're talking, this and that, and I'm doing my homework (sort of). Then they do a little of the parent stuff on me— are you doing your homework, are you going to get on the honor roll, your hair needs a washing, dada dada dada, sorta sweet, y'know? Then Ma notices that I'm getting a zit on my cheek and she zooms in on it. "What's this?" It looks like she's going to squeeze it. That does it!

Ka boom! I jumped up, tipped over my chair, started yelling. "Don't do that! Hands off!"

Ma says, "What? What did I do?" She looks all innocent and confused. You know how she gets

10

that look, like she's sorta blind behind her glasses? And Dad starts saying, "Now, Mouse. Now, Mouse."

So then they're both driving me crazy. And I say it, "You're driving me crazy!" And then they both get these really identical, sad, bewildered looks on their faces. And Daddy pats Ma's hand and says, *in front of me*, "She's only fifteen," as if fifteen is still thumb sucking and Pampers. And then—Jeremy, do you understand?—I'm ready to chew metal! I don't know what to say, where to start. I'm breathing hard, practically gnashing my teeth and Ma goes, "Oh . . . oh . . ." And this makes me even more berserk and I finish off this whole performance by running upstairs to my room and slamming the door. Only, I'm not through yet. I feel miserable. I'm pacing up and down, door to window, window to door, slapping myself on the forehead and telling myself, "Goddammit, Rachel! You don't know why you do the things you do. But you still do them."

And are you shaking your head, dear bro, at all this? At Rachel's awful behavior? Don't, don't, please don't! I don't want to be this way. Only, sometimes, they seem to get so much under my skin. I don't set out to make them sad or mad. So why do I? I don't know! Sometimes, I think—oh, God, I hate saying it, but it's true—*If only they weren't so old.*

I know, I know! That's no excuse for my vile temper. Jeremy, I tell you, there are times when I feel like I have this other thing, this *something*, that's living in me, messing around with me. I'm not trying to make excuses. It's there! Separate but united. Me and not me. D'ya know what I mean, Jerems? Does this make sense? I think of it

11

like a ghost, kind of soft and white, crouching in there, hiding from the light. Did I say soft? Oh, no, no, no, no. It's hard as a stone, it's like a fist in me, it knows what it wants, Jerems. It's down in there, crouching and shouting in that soundless voice that only I can hear: *Leave me alone. Don't treat me like a baby. Let go.* And then when it comes out, when I let it out (is that it?), I'm nearly always sorry, because it's a mess.

Thank you for letting me write this. Thank you for being there, for reading this. Hey, don't get a swelled head. I don't always thank you, Jeremy. Because sometimes I feel really hurt that you never write me back, except a postcard now and then. I know, you warned me a long time ago you weren't a letter writer, but I guess I keep hoping.

Love, your sister, Rachel

THREE

Lying on the floor on her back, Rachel considers the letter she has just written to her brother. Tomorrow she'll mail it. He ought to have it two or three days after that. For a week or two, maybe as much as a month—she knows herself—she'll come home from school every day, hoping there's a letter for her from Jeremy.

She ought to know better. She does, but she can't help hoping. Her total from-Jeremy mail consists of a handful of laconic postcards and less than a handful of letters. Three, to be exact, each one coming roughly three years apart. The first one arrived when Rachel was eight years old, as if Jeremy woke up one morning in Boston, remembered he had a sister, and wanted to make sure she remembered him. After that, silence again until she was eleven. He was in San Francisco then. Her third, latest letter from Jeremy is a mere six months old and postmarked New Orleans.

There are times when Jeremy's silence preys on Rachel, but mostly she forgives him everything. She thinks of him as the most—maybe the only—interesting person in the family. Jeremy Cooper, brilliant misfit.

"Jeremy's got it," her brother Phil told her the last

13

time he visited. "Do you know, Rachel, when that boy graduated high school, which he did in three years, his SATs were the highest of anybody on record?"

"Ma said a lot of colleges wanted him."

"Right. Harvard, Yale, and Swarthmore, to name just three."

"Why did he go to Reed?"

"That's what we all said. Not that it's not a good college. But Harvard!" Phil pulled at his soft, fat cheeks. "He wouldn't have to be a waiter right now if he'd graduated from Harvard. Well, knowing Jeremy, he might have ended up being the best-educated waiter in the United States."

Jeremy had stayed only a year in college, then dropped out. A year after that he was in Vietnam. He was there for three years.

"And never talked about it," Rachel's father says when the subject of Jeremy comes up, which is not too often, since it's an occasion of sadness for both of Rachel's parents.

"All right, when he came home, he needed to adjust from being in the war," Shirley says. "How long does it take to adjust? A year, two years, even four, that I could understand, but the boy has never adjusted. What that terrible war did to him, I don't know."

The "boy" is now thirty-five years old. He's had countless jobs, in all of which he performed brilliantly for six months to a year, then did something either stupid or perverse, which resulted in his being chastised, demoted, or fired. Truly, Rachel hardly knows him, since he was already on his way to Vietnam when she was born.

She knows her oldest brother, Phil, better. Even though he lives all the way across the country in

14

Spokane, Washington, with his family, Phil is a lot more knowable. He keeps in touch. He calls every month, and every couple of years they all come East to visit. In between visits there are photos, snapshots that Marilyn takes of the kids and Phil, and at New Year's there's always a formal group picture: a glossy eight-by-ten and several smaller prints of Phil, Marilyn, MB, and Taylor sitting in a photo studio with a big HAPPY NEW YEAR TO OUR WONDERFUL FAMILY! written across the bottom.

Phil is so much like a younger version of her father that when he visits, Rachel always finds herself helplessly, hopelessly loving him. Like her father, he is soft and fat and really good to everyone. He likes to send their mother presents—fruit baskets on her birthday, a surprise gift like a blouse or a scarf in the middle of the year, and a hefty check on her anniversary.

On her parents' last anniversary in March, Rachel took the picture that is now on her wall. In it, Manny and Shirley are sitting side by side on the couch, holding hands. The grizzle in Manny's hair doesn't show. Shirley is wearing red pants; Manny, a yellow shirt. They both look as relaxed as if they've just come back from a month's vacation in the sun. Manny and Shirley always take an excellent picture. So does Jeremy.

Rachel rolls over and studies the latest photo of Jeremy. Her walls are covered with newspaper clippings, drawings, pictures of musicians and writers, and family snapshots. Every year when Phil's family picture arrives, Rachel can see that her niece, MB, is taller, her nephew, Taylor, is bigger, and her brother Phil looks fatter and more uncomfortable.

But Jeremy's snapshots, which arrive with about the same frequency as his letters, show him almost unchanged. Twelve years ago he had long hair and a shaggy beard. He sported a headband, wore jeans and a fatigue jacket. This year he has long hair, a shaggy beard; the headband is gone, but the jeans are still present. The only variation on the theme has been wherever the photo is taken and whoever he's got his arm around—whoever is his current wife or love. For about the past year and a half, it's been New Orleans and Laurel.

Rachel unfolds her letter to Jeremy and rereads it. It's odd, but when she writes to Jeremy, she hardly ever anguishes the way she does when she writes in her journal. She writes whatever pops into her head. Maybe it's just because Jeremy never answers that she feels so free.

She pushes a pair of sneakers out of the way, spreads out the letter, and adds a few more lines.

P.S., Jerems, I read that New Orleans is called the City of Fun. Is it true that no people in the entire world know how to have as much fun as New Orleansites? Quick! Rush your answer!

What will he think when he reads this letter? She pictures him standing by a wrought-iron fence in front of a pink house, fronted by a tiny balcony with immense red flowers creeping all over it. She tries to peer through the fog in which Jeremy appears in her mind, to see what the expression is on his face. Thoughtful? Impatient? Or is he laughing at her? No, he's frowning, he's reading about the way she screamed at Shirley and Manny. Poor Shirley and Manny! Remorse covers Rachel. She scrambles to her feet and goes downstairs.

Her parents are in the living room, watching TV. Her mother is knitting. "Ma?" Rachel says. Shirley

16

looks up. Rachel can see in the softness of her mouth that she is still feeling hurt. "Sorry," Rachel says. It sounds grudging. She wants to be kinder, more generous, more lavish with her apologies, but everything dies in her throat.

"Oh . . . that's all right," her mother says.

It doesn't sound all right. Rachel lingers in the doorway. "What're you knitting?"

"A scarf for Grandpa Izzy. If he'll wear it." Shirley gives her a tiny, quivery smile, and Rachel crosses to her, bends, and kisses her quickly on the cheek.

"And me?" Manny says. "Don't I get something?" So Rachel kisses him on the cheek, too. Then they both smile at her, and she is free again.

"Helena, hi. What's up?" Rachel is sitting in the tiny, stifling closet under the stairs with the phone in her lap. She thought she had so much to say, but now that she's on the phone with Helena, she doesn't think she'll even mention the fight with her parents. Helena wouldn't understand. Not that she doesn't get exasperated with her parents, but she doesn't go crazy like Rachel.

Not to worry. If Rachel has nothing to say right now, Helena can always talk about Theater Club or the ongoing drama of her relationship with Mikey Shedds. Rachel once read that everyone has a counterpart in the animal world. If true, Helena looks like an amiable cat, round-faced and unflappable, while Mikey is another kind of cat, one of those young, handsome lions you always see on the nature shows, all blond mane and big, self-satisfied roars.

When Helena and Mikey got together last summer, it was like something out of a movie. Mikey was a lifeguard at Indian Lake State Park. Helena

17

was at the lake with her family. "I was just fooling around on the rubber raft with my little sisters," she told Rachel. "Then Tina fell off the raft and panicked. She came up screaming, and Mikey practically flew off the guard tower."

"He didn't jump off, did he?" Rachel asked.

"No, but the way he came down those steps, he might as well have. He was definitely out to rescue Tina."

"Well, what did you do?" Rachel said. "Let Tina drown so Mikey could rescue her?"

Helena slapped Rachel's arm. "Of course. Okay, okay, I had her up and out of the water by the time he arrived, but still . . . he was wonderful."

Helena goes up and down in her feelings about Mikey. Sometimes, everything he says, everything he does, is perfect, beyond reproach. Other times, Helena's full of doubts, even wants advice from Rachel. How can she get Mikey to tell her what he's feeling? Does Rachel think Mikey really loves her? Rachel doesn't want to let Helena down, but advice? From her? She's read plenty but knows nothing firsthand. She usually falls back on a judicious, "What do *you* think, Helena?"

This works surprisingly well. Helena always has something to say. And why not? She ought to know something about these things. She has had a boyfriend every year since she was in first grade. What must that be like? Rachel wonders. One year, in fifth grade, for two weeks, Rachel had a boyfriend. Thomas Leander. He showed up at her house every morning and walked to school with her. Then he moved away. In some part of her heart, Rachel still mourns the loss of Thomas Leander.

She leans her head against the slanted ceiling and listens to Helena. Maybe next time Rachel will talk and Helena will listen. Somehow, they almost always manage to balance each other. It's been this way, more or less, since that day two years ago when Helena linked her arm with Rachel's and said, "Let's eat lunch together."

"No," Rachel said, "you don't have to do that."

They were on their way out of the library. It was after Wilda Sycora spoke to their class. Rachel's face was still burning. Ten minutes earlier, when it was time for questions, she had been the first one on her feet. "Ms. Sycora"—saying "Ms." had been her first mistake—"Ms. Sycora, in your opinion, is it possible for someone young to break into the writing field? Or do you need to be experienced?"

That was her second mistake. The word *experienced* sent a wave of laughter sweeping over the room. It wasn't the first time her classmates had laughed at Rachel, but knowing that made it no easier to bear.

Rachel can't remember any longer what she did, if she sat down or continued standing up, as Wilda Sycora answered her question. What she does remember, as vividly as if it were happening all over again this moment, with the same pain in her stomach, with her cheeks again so hot they hurt, is the mocking laughter.

Wilda Sycora had paid no attention to that laughter, had looked only at Rachel and answered the question seriously and carefully, but Rachel's heart had been beating so ferociously, she could hardly hear the author.

It was when she was on the way out of the library that Helena Minor caught up with her. "Rachel, I really liked your question. Most of the other questions were so dumb. Did you hear Randy Burnet ask her how much money she made?"

19

Rachel had smiled politely. She knew Helena from some of her classes, a pretty, laughing girl who had always been carelessly friendly. "Hiii!" she'd say, passing Rachel in the hall. The same "Hiii!" she gave everyone. But now she took Rachel's arm. "Let's eat lunch together."

"No," Rachel said, stiffening. She read Helena's sudden interest in her as pity.

"Oh, come on," Helena said, not at all put off. "We can talk." She held Rachel's arm firmly.

Over the sloppy joe in the cafeteria, Rachel made an effort to set the record straight. "Look, this is very nice of you, but I know you just feel sorry for me because everybody laughed. Well, you don't have to. I'm fine."

"Sorry for you?" Helena shook her head. "No, that's not why I—" She broke off, looked straight at Rachel, and said, "Well, honestly, a little bit, that is true."

Rachel concentrated on her food. Helena's honesty hurt, but Rachel preferred it to hypocrisy.

"Anyway," Helena said, "I did like your question. You're different. I've wanted to know you, that's also the truth, so I just decided today was the day."

Rachel looked up. Unexpectedly, her throat tightened. "Well . . . thanks, then." She started to enjoy the lunch, sitting with Helena, laughing finally.

After that day, they were friendly—they did things together now and then, shopped, went to the movies—but they weren't yet real friends. They were just the least bit scratchy with each other. They seemed to do a little dance around each other, moving toward one another, then backing off. Maybe Helena had rushed into this too fast, Rachel thought. Or maybe it was her fault, because she was a little put off by Helena's attempts to improve her.

Helena wanted Rachel to wear makeup, smile more, not to show her brains quite so obviously.

"I don't like makeup. I smile enough. What can I do about my brains?" Rachel said. She was stubborn.

"You could flirt a little, it won't kill you."

"You mean, act dumb for a boy? Helena, that's depressing."

"Why? You know you're smart, that's what matters. Flirting just makes boys feel better."

"What's the matter with them? Why do they have to feel better by my pretending I'm dumber than they are?"

"It's just one of those things, Rachel."

"No. Forget it."

"Do you have to get that look on your face?"

"What look?"

"That look. The Look!" Helena did something with her face, lowering her brows, slitting her eyes. "This is you when you're annoyed."

"Oh, thank you. Something like a cross between a chimpanzee and a mad dog."

Oddly enough, the catalyst for sealing their friendship had been Rachel's Uncle Leonard, whom Rachel had never even met. Uncle Leonard was her mother's brother; he lived in London, England; and he was an actor. Rachel happened to mention this one day in connection with Helena's interest in acting. Helena was fascinated, went home with Rachel to look at the picture album, to see Leonard's picture: a short, gray-haired man with the same bulging eyes as Rachel's mother. "How lucky that he's your uncle!" Helena said. She stayed to talk, stayed to supper, stayed overnight.

"I like your room," she said when they went upstairs.

A winning remark. Rachel's room is her cave, her sanctuary. Her beloved refuge. Presumably, like most babies, she began her life sleeping in a crib, but she cannot remember a time before the maple four-poster bed with its worn pink-and-green quilt. There, to one side, is the sagging shelf with all her best childhood books, near it the gimpy rocking chair, and across from it the scratched old bureau. The walls are painted a soft blue; white net curtains hang at the window. Her room, always here, always waiting for her. When she's upset, crazy, morose, frantic, she comes here. Shut the door, the room says reassuringly. Crawl under the quilt with a book, the bed invites. Forget everything, the walls say soothingly.

"That bed is great," Helena had said. "You sure you want to give it to me?"

"Positive," Rachel said, unfolding the roll-away cot.

They talked for hours that night, woke up at the same moment the next morning, and brushed their teeth side by side in the bathroom. Helena borrowed a sweater, a scarf, and a bracelet from Rachel, and they went to school together. Friends that day. Friends ever after.

And still, such unlikely friends. Rachel: small, dark, brooding, taking everything to heart, everything too seriously. Helena: large and beautiful, bouncing with charm. Maybe it's just that old thing of opposites attracting.

"Rachel?" Helena says now. "I've been thinking about something."

The way Helena says this, with a little sweet drawl, alerts Rachel that Helena's about to switch into her missionary mode, her let's-improve-Rachel mode. "Helena, I'm not going to wear eye shadow,"

Rachel says firmly. "It makes me look as if someone punched me out."

"Rachel, I've given up on that. What I don't understand is why you don't have a boyfriend."

"Oh, that."

"Now, come on, you know you'd like a boyfriend. You can't pretend with me."

"Helena, I can't get one just by wanting one."

"That's exactly what I was thinking about. We should do something about this situation, Rachel."

"No, we shouldn't."

"Don't be difficult."

"I am difficult. Don't you know that by now? Anyway, I don't want a boyfriend, just to say I have one, like everyone else. And something else, maybe you can't miss what you haven't had."

"Well, haven't you ever had a boyfriend?"

"Please, Helena, this is painful. Do you want me to tell you about fifth grade and Thomas Leander again?"

Helena laughs. "Sure."

"Helena! I thought you were a nice person. I'm not telling you that stuff again. You get your kicks someplace else."

No, she has never had a real boyfriend. And if you don't count six kisses given her by runty Kevin Wertheim behind the smelly shower room at day camp (Rachel doesn't), or her parents, or Post Office and Spin the Bottle (Rachel doesn't), she has never been kissed, either. She would like to have that experience, at least, before her sixteenth birthday next April, or else she will have to go for her seventeenth. That begins to seem awfully old for a first kiss.

FOUR

Rachel is sitting in the library during seventh period, writing in her notebook. After a while she notices that her scalp is prickling; she has that shivery sensation that comes from being watched. She looks up and, sure enough, meets a pair of eyes across the room. Someone *is* watching her. Lewis Olswanger. Lewis Olswanger? Why is Lewis Olswanger watching Rachel Cooper? She knows him vaguely, he's in two of her classes, but she's hardly ever spoken to him. He is tall and thin, a narrow fellow; he has tight blond curls and large, prominent ears.

Maybe Lewis isn't watching her. Maybe he's watching Rhoda Rivers, who is sitting right across from Rachel. That makes a lot more sense. Rhoda Rivers is not only beautiful, with her masses of frizzy hair, but she nearly always wears something odd, different, or surprising. Today, she's tied ribbons around the arms of her blouse, above and below the elbows. She is an undeniably watchable girl. Alliance High is full of Rhoda Rivers watchers. Rachel understands, because she, herself, is a Rhoda Rivers watcher.

She stares at Rhoda. How can someone do something as ordinary as sit at a library table taking notes and still exude personality, charm, charisma? Whatever you call it, Rhoda's got it and Rachel hasn't. Of course, Rhoda is a senior, and that (Rachel hopes) could make some difference. But Rachel's real suspicion is that the Rhodas of the world were winners even as children.

Rachel goes back to her notebook. Today, she's not trying anything ambitious like a story. Instead, she's been working on a description of Mrs. Kayley, the librarian. "Wearing black boots and loose leather pants, she sits at her desk like a queen. She glances keenly at each subject who enters her domain—" But Rachel's concentration is ruined. Lewis Olswanger has ruined it.

She looks up. He's looking at her. Not at Rhoda Rivers. Definitely her. A boy is watching her. She grows warm, glows even. He looks something like Abraham Lincoln, she decides. Wrong color hair, but the ears are exactly right. Now, with the late-afternoon sun coming through the window behind him, those ears look like scalloped pieces of delicate pink glass.

He takes a small notebook out of his back pocket, checks something in it, then flips pages in a reference book. Only, his eyes aren't on the book. They're on her. She eases a mirror out of her purse and holds it in her lap. Maybe a miracle has taken place since the last time she looked. A transformation miracle.

Manny and Shirley always say she's pretty, "a pretty thing." She doesn't hold these little white lies against them. She would probably be disappointed if they didn't make those soothing noises in her direction, but it's impossible to believe them. They're her parents and they love her.

In the mirror she sees the merciless truth. She sees a pair of large, slightly bulging green eyes; a peaky little face; and wiry, impossible hair, which this morning she had braided six times. Now she has six ratty-looking plaits, leaking wires of hair in every direction.

She sneaks another look at Lewis. His ears are glowing, they've turned from pink to red and seem to give off sparks, as if on the verge of bursting into flames. She writes Lewis's name in tiny letters in a corner of her notebook. She sits up straighter. Should she smile? She fiddles self-consciously with her earrings. Maybe he'll come over to the table, sit down next to her, start a conversation. What should she say? Helena's warnings flare in her mind. Don't act smart. Okay, she won't say anything. No, that's awful. She'll talk. If he thinks she's too smart, too bad. Anyway, he's sure to think she's too short. She's got it all worked out—boys aren't attracted to her because she's short, and so they think she's younger and they're not interested. God, give me two more inches, she prays, even one, and then turn me loose.

Then the bell rings and Lewis Olswanger is gone like a streak of skinny lightning, out the door without a backward glance.

"Hello!" Izzy says.

"Hello, Grandpa."

About once a week, Rachel phones her grandfather. This is not something she looks forward to. Driving nails into cement is probably an easier chore than carrying on a conversation with Izzy.

"Who's this?" he says.

Why does he always ask that? "It's me, Rachel."

"Who?" He always says that, too.

"Ra-chel!"

"Oh, it's you. Why are you shouting? I'm not deaf."

"Sorry, I didn't mean—I just—" She stops, starts again. "Hi, Grandpa."

"Yes? Yes?" he says, as in, Yes? Yes? Why did you call?

A sigh wells up in Rachel's throat. "How are you, Grandpa?"

"How should I be?"

Rachel considers this question. Izzy is eighty-three—old, old, old—but his heart is strong, he's never broken a bone in his body, he walks four miles every day, and, as he likes to say, he's all set to go for another twenty years.

"I heard you had a stomachache," she says.

"Something disagreed with me," he concedes.

"And Ma took you to the doctor."

"Foolish."

"The doctor took blood or something?"

"Mmm-huh."

"Did you get the results?"

"Results? It's just a way for the doctor to make money."

There's a pause, during which Rachel searches for something else to say. Questions occur to her. What's it like being old? What do you do all day? I don't think you like me—is that true?

"So, you're feeling okay, Grandpa? The stomachache is gone?"

"Mmm-huh."

Hard going, but it isn't only Rachel who has trouble talking to Izzy. When Jeremy was home for a visit a couple of years ago, he said one of the reasons he'd come was to see his grandfather. He made a point of visiting Izzy alone one day, so that they could spend time together. From that visit, Jeremy, bold Jeremy with his beautiful shaggy beard and sad brown eyes, came back white-faced and shaking.

Actually shaking because Grandpa Izzy had told him off, no mercy given.

"What's this crazy life you're leading?" Izzy had said. "You get married, you get divorced, you get married, you get divorced, you go from one woman to another. Do you think you're an Arab sheikh? You don't have children, you go from one job to another like a jackrabbit. Is that a way for a man to live? No. It's a life for a selfish boy." And then he had delivered his verdict, like a curse on Jeremy. "You're too old now, the time is gone. You've lost your chance for a decent life."

Years ago, long before Rachel was born, something also happened with her Uncle Leonard and Grandpa Izzy, some kind of quarrel because Leonard wanted to go into the theater. From the things Rachel has heard, her grandfather's attitude was: Either you do it my way, son, or you don't do it. So her uncle left home when he was younger than Rachel is now, shipped out on a boat as a deckhand, jumped ship in England, and stayed there. The only time he came back was for his mother's funeral. That, too, was before Rachel was born, in another life that she didn't share.

Every once in a while, Rachel's mother gets really sad about not ever seeing her baby brother, but she doesn't blame Izzy. "Grandpa was brought up differently," she says. "He wasn't born in this country. He doesn't understand about people like Jeremy and my brother Lenny. Grandpa was brought up that you should get a trade and stick with it, you should get married and stay married, that you should take a job, work hard, and keep that job. He doesn't understand about things like finding yourself, or being an actor, or trying out new ideas."

Maybe, Rachel thinks, and maybe not. Grandpa's

no dope, he could try harder to understand. She can't forget that he talked to her brother Jeremy as if he were some kind of scummy lowlife. *You've lost your chance for a decent life.* How come Grandpa has to have his own way all the time? Be a bully? Say anything he wants to everybody?

Does she have nothing positive to say about Grandpa Izzy? Well, he's not, as her mother says all the time, a complainer. Also, he's independent and he's got all his marbles.

"So, Grandpa," she says, "did you watch any good TV shows this week?"

"Except for the news, junk, all junk."

"Which ones?"

"What's the point of discussing trash?"

"Guess you're right. . . . Did you go for a walk today?"

"Of course."

And another pause ensues, even longer than the first one.

"Are you still there, Grandpa?"

"I haven't left yet."

"Well . . . I should go do some homework."

"Good-bye, then." Click, and he's off.

"Good-bye," she says to the empty line.

FIVE

"I've never played paddleball," Rachel says as she slides into the backseat of the Minors' BMW. "Hi, Helena. I'm not even sure what paddleball is. Do you paddle a ball, or what? Is it like Ping-Pong?" Nervousness makes her talk too much. "Hello, Mr. Minor. Hello, Mrs. Minor. Helena, are you sure about this? Maybe I should just get out and take a rain check or something."

"You're going to do fine." Helena pulls up her white wool socks. She's wearing a heavy white cable-stitch sweater, navy pants, white sneakers. Rachel quickly checks out her own outfit—green cords, brown wool sweater, tan windbreaker. Definitely not great, like Helena's.

"Paddleball's really not a hard game to pick up," Mrs. Minor says.

"Am I dressed okay?" Rachel says to Helena.

"You can wear anything to play paddle. Stop worrying. You're going to get enough of a handle on the game to have fun right away."

"Helena. You're talking to the original uncoordinated kid. I'm lucky I learned to skip rope. The only Cooper I know of who isn't totally unathletic is my brother Jeremy. There are rumors he voluntarily plays basketball every Saturday."

In the front seat, Mr. Minor chuckles. This gives

Rachel a nice little heart palpitation. Helena's father is so handsome! Rachel appreciates greatly that she's sitting where she has an excellent view of his profile. "Too bad it's so warm today," he says. "The best play is when it's around twenty."

"No, when it goes down to about ten," Mrs. Minor says.

"Degrees?" Rachel says, getting a laugh out of the Minors. Only, she was serious. But so are they.

"This is an outside game," Mr. Minor instructs, turning around, "and the best time to play it is when it's cold. The ball is perfect then."

"Ahh," Rachel says. She has never really understood people who do all these healthy, beneficial, cold things.

"Do you do any winter sports, Rachel?" Mr. Minor asks.

"Biggest winter sport in our family is keeping warm." She gets another laugh.

Helena nudges her. "What'd you do last night?"

"The usual. How about you? Mikey?"

"Right. We went to the movies. You should have seen him, Rache. He was wearing a new blue sweater. Looked supremely gorgeous." Since her parents are right there, Helena doesn't say anything else.

Mrs. Minor pulls up in front of the paddleball courts. Getting out of the car, Rachel eyes the courts uneasily. They look like enormous bird cages. They are half-size tennis courts on raised platforms, enclosed by twelve-foot-high wire fences. Okay, she tells herself, it's going to be an experience, and everybody knows writers need experience.

Mrs. Minor hands Rachel a wooden racket with holes in it. The two of them play against Helena and Mr. Minor. "We keep score just like tennis, Rachel,"

Mrs. Minor says, as if Rachel knows any more about tennis than she does about paddleball. "Move up to the net when I do, Rachel . . . that's the way . . . Good try!" Helena's mother encourages Rachel, compliments her every time she does something even vaguely right. But they keep losing games, anyway. It's Rachel's fault, she knows it's her fault.

She wonders if she ought to apologize, although Helena's mother doesn't seem to mind a bit. When Rachel makes a particularly inept move, swinging the racket and missing the ball by a mile, Mrs. Minor laughs and makes a joke of it, showing splendid, big white teeth. If Rachel were about three years younger, she'd have a crush on Mrs. Minor. As it is, she smiles weakly and tries even harder. But they still lose every game.

Later, while Mr. and Mrs. Minor play another set with friends, Rachel and Helena sit in the Hut, a little room between the two courts. Helena breaks out cans of soda and opens a bag of corn chips. "Isn't it fun?" she says.

"Yes, but I'm such a klunk."

"You're not! Don't say things like that. Don't put yourself down."

"I know. Smile, smile, smile."

"Well, it doesn't hurt. Anything interesting happen in school yesterday?"

"Such as?" Rachel says, although she immediately thinks of Lewis Olswanger.

"Anything," Helena says.

"Well, there was one little thing."

"Yes?" Helena leans forward.

"No big deal, but it was sort of nice." She tells Helena about Lewis, starting from the beginning with that shivery feeling down her neck. She takes her time telling the story, puts in Rhoda Rivers, her doubts, Lewis's ears, all the little details.

Before she finishes, it's time to go and they let it drop. So it's not until Helena stops off at Rachel's house that Rachel gets around to telling her about the way Lewis Olswanger left the library.

They're outside, Rachel's raking leaves, and Helena's sitting cross-legged on the picnic table, under the Norway maple.

"That's it?" Helena says. "He just left like that? He only looked at you? He didn't speak to you? He didn't say anything to you? Nothing?"

"Well, he was all the way across the room," Rachel says, leaning on the rake.

"Oh, big excuse. If he wanted to talk to you—"

"We don't know that," Rachel says. "All we know is that he was staring at me. Maybe he got me mixed up with someone else."

"No," Helena says, "he didn't."

"Maybe he's nearsighted."

"No," Helena says, "he's not."

"Maybe he's researching library usage, counting the number of females at each library table."

"No," Helena says, "he isn't."

"How come you're so knowledgeable?"

Helena rocks a little. There's a satisfied expression on her round, pretty face. "Well, Rache, I might as well tell you. I was talking about you."

A wind blows across the yard, blows through the heaps of leaves. Rachel freezes. She hates people to talk about her. She doesn't know why; it's just something in her nature. "Talking about me?"

"Uh-huh," Helena sings out teasingly. "Talk, talk, talk."

"Why?"

33

"Why? What do you mean, why? Don't you want to know *who* I was talking to about you?" Then Helena answers herself. "Lewis and Mikey."

"Lewis *Olswanger?*"

"Uh-huh," Helena sings out again. Her smile grows bigger. "Rachey, he's Mikey's cousin." She watches Rachel with a mischievous look, waiting for that to sink in. "He came over to my house the other day with Mikey, didn't say a word the whole time. Funny boy! And I thought of you. And I said your name."

Rachel gathers an armful of leaves and shoves them into a plastic bag. "My name? That's all you said? All that staring and gawking just because you said my name?"

"Well . . . no, I admit I did a bit more than that. Lewis said he knew you, and I said, of course, he knew you. Everybody knows you. Then, you know, I did a little PR." Helena holds up her hand, Girl Scout fashion. "But only the truth! I said what a great person you are, how smart and funny. I said you were really intelligent. I figured that would get Lewis interested, because he's a pretty smart guy himself. You know, Mikey and I talked it over later, and we think you two are the perfect match."

"Oh, Helena! I wish you hadn't said anything. It makes me feel like a specimen."

"But, Rachel—are you mad? It's only because I love you. Here I am with Mikey, and here you are with no one. It's not fair. And Lewis has no one, either."

Rachel doesn't know what to say. She's really embarrassed, plus a little angry. Lewis Olswanger had been primed. It wasn't her, Rachel, who caught his attention; it was remembering that his cousin's girlfriend had practically begged him to give poor, boyfriendless Rachel Cooper a little attention.

Oh, forget it, she tells herself. Lewis Olswanger is nothing to her. Less than nothing. If he were to materialize this moment in front of her, she wouldn't spare him a single glance. If he were to beg her to talk to him, she'd sweep past him as if he were invisible. If he fell down on his hands and knees in front of her and groveled, she'd step over him as disdainfully as if he were no more than a heap of dried-up leaves. She shoves another armful of leaves into the bag and steps down on them. Then she closes the bag and twists it into a knot, with as much satisfaction as if it were Lewis's neck between her hands.

SIX

"Do we walk or take the car to Grandpa Izzy's?" Manny says on Sunday morning.

It's about a mile and a half to Emerson Street where Izzy lives, but every Sunday it's the same question, walk or drive, as if everyone doesn't already know the answer. Rachel's parents drive. She walks. Once in a very great while, if it's not too hot or too cold, too dry or too wet, too windy or too breezy, they will all walk there together.

Rachel's parents have been getting ready to leave for at least an hour, putting together food and carrying bags out to the car. She knows that even when they're ready, they'll both still be looking around to see if they forgot anything. And when they're finally in the car, her mother will have to get out again and go back inside to make sure she locked the front door and didn't leave any gas jets open on the stove.

"Well, what's the weather? Any better?" Rachel's mother looks out the window. "Uh-oh, it's raining now."

Manny is changing his shoes. He stops to look out the window, too. "Cold and wet," he pronounces.

"Oh, we can't walk in this weather."

"I can," Rachel says on cue. She takes a jacket from the closet.

"I don't want you catching a cold."

36

"It's chilly," her father says.

"At least put a scarf around your neck." Her mother finds a scarf, hands it to Rachel, watches as she drapes it over her neck. "You could drive with us."

"Plenty of room," her father says.

"I need the exercise. Teenagers are getting flabby, it's a national health problem."

She makes her getaway to the sound of their laughter. They love it when she jokes with them, even such a feeble little joke. They are so easily pleased that she feels guilty, but a dash of guilt isn't nearly enough to get her to give up her walk to her grandfather's. She stuffs the scarf into her pocket. She loves walking. If walking were a sport, she might even be a champion. The only thing she doesn't like about walking are the dogs. Though she's ashamed to admit it, Rachel is afraid of dogs and has worked out a nearly dogless route to her grandfather's house. The two dogs she encounters are—for dogs—friendly and, even better, fenced in.

Izzy lives in an apartment complex, the Loren Towers. The name sounds elegant, vaguely English, but the Loren Towers are three five-story brick buildings, serviceable and with no frills. Rachel waits in the downstairs lobby of *C* Building for her parents. It's a small, bare room with a couple of wooden benches, flat rows of mailboxes, and a community bulletin board. A sign on the board reads, PLEASE HELP KEEP THIS BUILDING CLEAN. DO NOT SPIT ON THE FLOOR. DOGS AND BARE FEET NOT ALLOWED.

A woman with crooked legs and deeply waved purple hair passes Rachel on her way to the elevator. "Hello, darling."

"Hi," Rachel says. She doesn't know the woman,

but she's seen her before. A lot of older people live in the Loren Towers.

Here come her parents. She watches them approach, walking up the curved sidewalk, each of them with a grocery bag in their arms.

"So you got here ahead of us, Rachey," her father says, as if she doesn't always arrive first. "Fast walker, our daughter."

Then the two of them take the elevator, and Rachel takes the stairs to the fourth floor. They all arrive at the same time.

"This elevator is so slow," Shirley says. "And it wheezes! We should walk up like Rachey. Let's use the stairs next week, Manny. It's good for the heart." They proceed down the corridor to Izzy's apartment.

"Hello, Daddy, isn't it a wonderful day outside?" Rachel's mother says as Izzy opens the door to them. She kisses her father and, with a finger in the small of Rachel's back, pushes her forward to kiss him, too.

Rachel catches a whiff of toothpaste and onions. Izzy is a big, bulky man with wild gray eyebrows. His hands are broad, grayish from cement, and still strong-looking, although it's been almost twenty years since he has worked as a stonemason. His teeth are stained from years of smoking and some of them are gone, but the skin on his arms is still remarkably smooth. Today, the apartment is hot and he wears his shirt sleeves rolled up like a boy.

"Brought you the paper, Dad," Rachel's father says. Rachel and her mother put the bags of food into the tiny kitchen.

The living room is bare and clean. A table, chairs, a TV, a small bookcase, an old gray couch. Two windows facing west get afternoon sun. Rachel's parents and her grandfather sit down.

"Well. Here we are, all together. Isn't this nice?" Rachel's mother says.

Izzy grunts, pats his pockets. Back pockets, front pockets, then back pockets again.

"Daddy," Shirley says, "what are you looking for? Maybe I can help you."

"When I need you to help me find something in my own house, I'll let you know. I'm not senile yet."

"No kidding. Everybody should have the memory you do."

Izzy fishes a folded dollar bill out of his shirt pocket. He's breathing hard as he holds it out to Shirley. "For the gas."

She puts her hands behind her back. "I don't want your money, Daddy. I can take you to the doctor without . . . This is ridiculous, I only took you downtown."

"And the parking?"

"Daddy, the parking! So what! Manny." She appeals to Rachel's father. "Tell him we don't want his money."

"Take it, Shirl."

"Manny!" Shirley looks from her father to her husband. "We don't need his money."

"I didn't say we did."

"Also your time—" Izzy stops, holds his hand to his side, as if he's got a stitch there. "Your time's worth something," he says irritably.

"My time! Daddy, if I can't take an hour to drive my own father to the doctor . . ."

Rachel peeks at her watch. Only ten minutes have passed and already she's antsy, torn between pity and impatience at how nervous her mother is around her grandfather, how she's always hovering over him and trying to please him.

The money matter is finally settled when Shirley

agrees to let Izzy buy the gas next time. He sits down on a chair with his hands flat on his thighs. "Well, Manny?"

"I'm good, Dad."

"Mmm-huh." Izzy pops his bridge out of his mouth, then back in.

Manny folds his hands over his stomach. "No complaints from my side. And you, Dad?"

"Eh! This week, not so good. These stomach cramps. And a little short of breath sometimes . . . but that's nothing. You see me here, don't you?"

"How old are you now?"

"Eighty-three," Shirley says proudly.

"Eighty-two," Izzy says.

"No, Daddy, eighty-three. Last April you were eighty-three."

"Eighty-two."

"Daddy, I'm sure—"

"How come you know my age better than me?"

Izzy has always had strong opinions on everything from blood pressure (nobody's going to stop me from eating salt) to labor unions (they're good) to women's rights (they've got everything they want, don't they?). But he's grown more rough-edged with time. Food, weather, and health are usually the only safe subjects for conversation. He's developed that habit of popping his bridge in and out of his mouth, then flexing his lips as he adjusts the bridge. And sometimes when they come to visit, he's got the windows open, it's cold in the apartment, and he says, "It's good for you!" So they sit, shivering, while he's wearing layers of clothes—a couple of shirts, two or three sweaters—all shabby, all coming unraveled at the edges.

"Sit down, Rachey," her father says now. "Be comfortable, sweetheart."

"I'm okay." She's leaning against the wall, arms folded. Her grandfather glances at her. It makes her feel uncomfortable. What is he thinking?

"Did you call the doctor, Daddy?" Shirley says.

Izzy's wild eyebrows go up. "If he's got something to say, he'll call me, Shirley."

"Well, somebody has to call somebody. He did tests and we have to know—"

"I told you, all I had was a little indigestion. I ate raw onions. They always affect me that way."

"Yes, but you still have those pains, don't you?"

"I'll be around after you're gone, Shirley."

Rachel shifts her feet. Her grandfather's boasting is hard to take. It sounds like he wouldn't mind if her mother died.

Her mother must have heard it that way, too. Her nose reddens and she glances away from Izzy, as if she doesn't want to hurt him by letting him see the hurt in her eyes. "How's your appetite, Daddy?" she says.

Every week she asks about Izzy's appetite. Every week he says, "My appetite is good. I enjoy my food."

"My appetite is good. I enjoy my food."

Now Rachel's father and grandfather will exchange a few words about Manny's work. Then her mother will get anxious about her grandfather's health. Shouldn't he have his blood pressure checked again? It was a little high last time. And how did he sleep?

Rachel waits.

"How did you sleep, Daddy?" her mother says. "Are you sleeping okay?"

Now he will say, "I never have trouble sleeping. I can sleep anywhere."

"I never have trouble sleeping. I can sleep anywhere. I can sleep on the floor. I can sleep on the ceiling if I have to."

"Aren't you lucky!" Shirley jumps up and kisses her father again. The blush from her nose has spread to her cheeks, her eyes grow moist, and Rachel is startled into thinking she knows how her mother must have looked when she was fourteen—big brown eyes and pretty.

The talk goes on. A movie none of them will see. The price of eggs. Rachel takes another peek at her watch. Pretty soon she and her mother will retreat into the kitchen to make a meal. Cooking the meal with her mother is the nicest part about visiting Izzy. Rachel actually likes this part very much, which is perverse of her, since at home, she'll do anything to avoid working in the kitchen.

But at Grandpa Izzy's, it's somehow different. The two of them in the little kitchen can't help running into each other, and they laugh a lot and cook too much food, recklessly, as if they're in a conspiracy against her grandfather and father. "Now, you boys have to eat everything on the table," Rachel's mother jokes.

She's convinced hers is the one decent meal Izzy has all week. Today it's roasted chicken, baked potatoes with sour cream, carrots in honey, and a big green salad she tries to persuade Izzy to eat.

"Don't bother me," he says, bringing the pickle jar to the table. He holds the sodden pickle over his plate. "Your mother tried to get me to eat good for forty-five years, Shirley, and she didn't succeed, so how are you going to make me do anything?"

Later, the sun is out again and they all go out to the zoo. They stroll around, looking at the animals. Izzy has a paper bag with stale bread. He sits down on a bench and feeds the pigeons.

At the monkey cages, her mother presses Rachel's arm. "Rachey, you know what? First on my list that I wanted to be when I was a young girl, before I married your father, was a lawyer."

"I didn't know that."

"She was going to be another Clarence Darrow," Izzy scoffs.

Shirley laughs. "Right. And if I couldn't be that, second on my list was a zookeeper, but especially a monkey keeper."

"Shirl," Manny says, lighting a cigar, "I'd say you got that part of your wish."

And then, like a band of light wrapping around the four of them, they all look at each other and laugh.

SEVEN

Rachel hates getting up in the morning. Does anyone care? No. Her father clumps through the house, turns on the radio, yells to her mother, "Shirl, where's my blue shirt?"

And her mother, rushing up the stairs so she can wake Rachel, yells back, "It's in the dryer, honeybunch." A moment later, she is in Rachel's room, tugging off the covers. "Come on, Rachey, up, up."

In the bathroom, Rachel splashes cold water on her face and thinks how unfair it is to make everybody go to school at the same time. Some people are larks. Some people are owls. She is an owl. More cold water.

Downstairs, there's a full breakfast laid out. "You have five minutes," Shirley says. "Eat." Rachel doesn't even like to *look* at food in the morning. She takes two tiny bites of egg to make her mother happy.

She runs all the way to school. It'll be a miracle if she gets there. But every Monday, it's a miracle she gets to school at all. She crosses the street, runs up the stairs, pushes through the front door, and smashes head-on into Lewis Olswanger.

It's like something out of a teen romance! His books go flying. His papers scatter like confetti.

They both scramble around, grabbing stuff and muttering apologies to each other. They're on their hands and knees, Rachel is stuffing his papers back into Lewis's arms, they're looking into each other's eyes, and—it's perfect.

In a story, she would know, right now, that he's the one, *the guy*. The only thing lacking is the wave of sizzling electricity Rachel should be feeling. Girls are always feeling waves of sizzling electricity when they see *the guy*. And they can always tell who he is, because they do dumb things like Rachel just did, crashing into Lewis and knocking his books to beyond.

Wait! Here it comes! But it's not a wave of electricity she feels smashing into her belly like a fist, it's a wave of nausea. She scrambles up, dropping a book on Lewis's foot, and runs faster than she ran all the way to school, hand over mouth, to the nurse's office. She arrives barely in time to throw up into the sink.

Mrs. Brandor, the nurse, pulls Rachel's hair back behind her face and hands her a wet towel to sponge with. "Feeling a little sick, are you?" she says in a jolly manner. Everyone calls her Brandy. A thin little woman with clay-colored skin and big circles under her eyes, she looks like a candidate for the intensive care unit.

"I never get sick," Rachel says.

"Probably the flu. Keep eating. Too many people stop eating when they get sick. But if you stick to light food, crackers, boiled eggs—"

The word *egg* makes Rachel heave again. "Not sick," she whispers, hanging on to the sink. "Never get sick."

"Good for you. Better lie down for a while."

Rachel totters over to the cot. "I'll be okay in a few minutes." She pulls the thin brown blanket over her shoulders and starts shaking.

Brandy takes her temperature, then writes a note on a chart, just like somebody out of *General Hospital.* "Afraid we have to send you home. Can someone come get you?"

Rachel half sits up. Not her parents. They'll just get upset. "I don't know . . . let me think." She falls back on the cot. It's amazing how suddenly she has no strength, how uttering those few words leaves her feeling exhausted and about a hundred years old. Did she run all the way to school? It seems to have happened four or five weeks ago, somewhere back in the good old days, when she was young and strong.

Rachel is half awake, or half asleep, when she hears the door open, hears footsteps, then a male voice saying, "Did, uh, Rachel Cooper come in here?"

"She's right there," Brandy says. "You've been in here before, too. You're—" She snaps her fingers. "Something like olives . . . Olswanger," she says triumphantly. "Sure, you're the splinter in the thumb, came in here last week, right?"

"Right."

Brandy laughs. "And your friend is the upchuck in the sink."

Rachel lies like a mummy, trying in true mummy fashion to neither shake nor breathe. She's not sick, she's dead. She's gone from this world. She's just a hunk of bones lying on the cot, waiting for burial. She will never have to look at Lewis Olswanger again, never have to see him thinking, She's the upchuck in the sink.

Rachel is sick all week. By Thursday, her fever is gone, but she still has no strength. One good thing about being sick, every morning her mother brings her breakfast on a tray and doesn't say a word when Rachel passes up the boiled eggs.

"I'm bringing Grandpa into the hospital for some tests today," Shirley says, Friday morning, sitting on the edge of Rachel's bed. "The doctor called, he wants to check some things. He'll keep Grandpa in overnight."

Rachel remembers Izzy's stomach pains. "Does he have the flu, too?" She feels a certain kinship for a fellow sufferer.

"Yes, some kind of stomach virus," Shirley says. "You're lucky you're getting better so fast. It takes longer for older people."

"I'm still sick," Rachel says defensively, pulling up the covers. Later, though, she gets out of bed, showers, dresses, and writes in her journal. The next morning, she feels completely normal and goes with her mother to the hospital to pick up her grandfather.

He's waiting for them in his room. "What took you so long? I've had enough of this place."

"The doctor said to wait for him, didn't he?" Rachel's mother looks around the room. "You took all your stuff, Daddy?"

Izzy goes to the door. "Doctors are never on time." He's breathing hard and there's a light film of sweat on his face. He paces up and down, his arms crossed over his stomach. "He said ten o'clock. He's half an hour late."

"No, Daddy, it's only ten-fifteen."

Just then, the doctor strolls in. He's a tall, cherubic-looking man in a camel-hair jacket. "Hello, folks." Smiling, he shakes Izzy's hand. "Chomping at the bit to go home, are you?"

"What about the tests, Doctor?" Shirley says.

"Give the man a chance, let him talk," Izzy says.

The doctor puts his hand on Izzy's shoulder. "Mr. Shapiro, your tests are fine, you have a little virus right now that may hang on for a while. Don't worry about it. Go home, eat, rest, enjoy yourself. Do what you feel like doing." He scribbles on a prescription pad. "I'll give you something for any discomfort you might feel. You can take one of these every four hours. Call me if you think you need to." He holds out the slip of paper.

"Give it to my daughter, Doc. She'll take care of it."

When he talks to the doctor, Rachel hears something different in her grandfather's voice, an almost humble quality. As they walk to the elevator, he looks around uneasily and allows her mother to take his arm. If she didn't know Izzy better, she might almost think he's afraid.

EIGHT

On Monday, late in the day, Rachel stops into the dispensary to interview Brandy for a feature article she's writing for the school newspaper on the non-classroom staff. "Sure you can interview me," Brandy says. "If you ask me, you look a hell of a lot perkier than you did last time I saw you."

"I guess so," Rachel says, and that's when she remembers—but only vaguely—Lewis Olswanger showing up in the dispensary. She was feverish and can't remember why he was there, only that something about the memory is unpleasant. But what?

It's not until the next morning when she walks into the school office and sees Lewis's tall, thin figure standing at the desk that she remembers. Oh, no, she thinks, and starts backing out of the office.

"Yes, Miss Cooper?" Mrs. Trudy says.

Lewis's head swings around.

"Uh, nothing," Rachel says. "I forgot my locker key, but that's all right."

"You forgot your key also?" Mrs. Trudy says. She has a very loud voice. "What is this, an epidemic?" She takes the master key off a board and hands it to Rachel. "Okay, I entrust you with this, Miss Cooper. Give it to Mr. Olswanger when you're done. But you return it."

Rachel and Lewis walk to the lockers in silence.

She'd say something if she could think of something to say. The trouble is, all she can think of is what Brandy said about her. "The upchuck in the sink." That pert little phrase has wiped out her brains. In silence she uses the master key, in silence she waits while Lewis opens his locker, and in silence she takes the key back from him.

Later, she remembers that the reason he was in the dispensary was to ask about her. She should have said something. Thank you . . . that was nice of you . . . sorry I dropped a book on your foot. . . . On the other hand, he didn't say anything at the lockers, either. No surprise. What is there to say to a girl you're thinking of as the upchuck in the sink?

Please, just stay out of my way, she prays silently, passing Lewis in the hall later that day. But her prayer must have gone astray. Or else she said it the wrong way. Because for the rest of the week, in some kind of cosmic joke, Lewis shows up everywhere Rachel does.

That very afternoon, she goes into the library after school, just as Lewis is coming out. This time he says, "Hi." So she does, too.

Wednesday morning, early, she drops into the school newspaper office in the basement to talk to Ted Pickens, the editor, about the article she's working on. No, Lewis is not there, but he's in the next room. "Olswanger," she overhears clearly as she walks past, "is going to try his hand at getting some ads for the paper. Is that right, Olswanger?"

Thursday. Lunch hour. The sun is shining and Rachel goes outside to eat. She's not the only one with this idea. There's a vast throng of kids milling around the front steps and sitting on the stone wall. People are playing Frisbee and touch football on the lawns.

Rachel heads for her own favorite spot, an out-of-the-way corner near the parking lot. She'll put her back against the warmed brick wall, eat her sandwich, and read her book. It's called *Frost in Winter*, it's about another time, another place, and a girl from a family utterly unlike hers. Rachel loves it. As she rounds the corner, she trips over someone's outstretched feet, someone's large, scruffy white sneakers. Even before she looks up, even as she's recovering herself and automatically saying, "Oh, sorry," even before she hears the other person—this person who's taken her special place—mumble his apologies, "No, my big feet," she *knows*.

Lewis Olswanger grins feebly at her. "Sorry."

"Me, too." She walks on by, keeps going right around the corner.

But that's not all. Over the weekend, the D'Oyly Carte Company is at the Civic Center to perform *H.M.S. Pinafore*. Rachel's father is a fan of D'Oyly Carte. He has all the D'Oyly Carte albums and has never missed a performance when they come to town. It's been a tradition, for years, for Rachel to go with him.

This year, she would like not to go. She has several reasons, not the least being that every year, just as they get in the car, her father says, "Well, Mouse, going on a date with your daddy?" She doesn't think she wants to hear that again. She knows she's socially retarded. Does she have to be reminded of it?

Then there are all the other rites that will take place, the things they do every year and will surely do again this year. Going out after the show to eat huge banana splits. Singing Gilbert and Sullivan on the drive home. (Rachel, with her tin ear, following Manny's wheezy bass: "I'm called Little Buttercup—dear Little Buttercup, though I could never tell why . . .") And listening to her father telling her stories about Gilbert and Sullivan.

"It was Gilbert who wrote the lyrics for the operas, Rachey." (She knows that.) "Sullivan wrote the music. Now think about this, Rachel, they wrote these operettas more than a hundred years ago and people still get pleasure out of them." (Every year she thinks about that.) "Rachey, did I ever tell you the story about Gilbert being kidnapped?" Of course he has. Every single year.

"You see, he wasn't kidnapped because he was the famous Gilbert. It happened a long time before that, when he was just a baby. His parents were wealthy, very rich. They had to pay twenty-five pounds—English money, of course—to have him returned. At that time, it was quite a sum of money. They say that experience affected him. When he grew up, he had everything, he was handsome, talented, famous. And you know what?"

"What?" (She knows.)

"Gilbert turned out to be a *terrible person* who quarreled with everyone."

And finally, after the performance and after the banana splits and the stories, she and her father will creep into the house, bent over like two cartoon characters, tiptoe with elaborate care through the dark kitchen, into the dining room, through the swinging door, and into the little front hall with its three-legged table, ornate mirror, and old black phone.

"Shh, shhh, shhh," Manny will say. "Your mother. Shh. We don't want to wake her up." But Shirley is never asleep. She always waits up for them, and Manny always produces a carton of ice cream he's brought for her. And she always acts surprised. And they always sit down and eat the ice cream with her, and Manny always says, "Oh, we shouldn't be doing this. If you could have seen what Mouse and I had already, you'd be shocked." And he always looks at Rachel and he always winks.

"So, Dad," Rachel says that morning while they're eating breakfast, "maybe I won't go with you this evening." She keeps her voice casual. "I'll save you some money."

"What are you talking about, Rachel? I have the tickets already. We've planned this for months."

"Ma could go with you, Dad."

"That's not my kind of music," her mother says. "I like Tony Martin."

"Sweetheart," her father says, "what's the matter, you don't want to go with me?" And he looks so disappointed, Rachel lets the whole thing drop.

That evening, after supper, getting ready to go out, she starts thinking about MB Cooper, her niece. MB, Phil's daughter, is only three months younger than Rachel but a head taller and, in this last year, has suddenly come to look at least three years older. MB and her little brother, Taylor, had flown from Spokane to visit over the winter holidays. As usual, MB slept in Rachel's room. They had always been friendly enough, though MB never liked that Rachel was her aunt. "It makes you seem too old," she would complain. But now, something else came between them. Socially, MB seemed to have made giant leaps beyond Rachel.

Touching the tiny silver unicorns in her ears, MB had said, "Brian gave them to me."

"Who's he?"

"One of my boyfriends."

"One?" Rachel said.

"Want to see something?" She pulled down her jeans and showed Rachel a tiny rose tattooed on her thigh. "My mother would kill me if she knew. I did it for Jeffy."

Now, as Rachel slips a long, beaded earring into one ear and a gold hoop into the other, she sighs and reflects that if, way across the country in Spokane, MB is going out tonight, it sure isn't with her daddy.

"So, Mouse," her father says as she settles herself into the car. "Going out on a date with your old father again."

"Dad, how old are you?"

"Ahh, compared to your grandfather, not that old. But compared to how old I used to be, very old!" He laughs at his own joke.

Downtown, he lets her out in front of the Civic Center. "I'll find parking, you go ahead," he says.

Their seats are first-row balcony. She sits down, takes off her jacket. The orchestra is tuning up. There's the buzz of people entering, the sparkle of the lights, the fresh, crisp smell of her program. Rachel starts feeling glad that she's here.

"Excuse me," someone says. Rachel stands to allow him to pass and—no, this is not possible. Lewis Olswanger sits down three seats away from her.

"Well," Lewis says, looking at her, raising bony shoulders, "it must be fate."

Rachel taps her program against her lips. Is there anything to do when fate overtakes you? Except give in? "You're probably right," she says. And they smile at each other.

NINE

On Monday evening, Rachel's parents go out to visit friends and she's home alone. She washes her hair, wraps it in a towel, turban fashion. She likes being in the house alone, likes the quiet, familiar sounds—floors creaking, the furnace humming, a clock ticking. Outside, it's cool, the wind is blowing and leaves patter down on the roof. All this begins a poem in her head: "You wonder where/You listen here/And all the years/And leaves and leaves and leaves . . ."

Downstairs, she puts on a record, an old Beatles record that was Jeremy's, and lies on the living-room floor, writing in her journal. First the poem. Then a new page and the start of another letter to Jeremy.

Dear Jeremy,

Have you ever noticed how sometimes it seems impossible to be happy and other times, it's so easy? Right now, I'm happy because 1. My hair is clean, 2. I just started a poem, 3. I'm writing to you, and, oh, yes, 4. If I feel like it, I can sing and no one's here to say, "Oh, Rachel's tin ear!"

The phone rings in the kitchen. "Good evening, Ms. Cooper. This is Ron Heartbroker of Station

WTIC. I have three trivia questions for you, Ms. Cooper—"

"Uh, no thanks, I don't—"

"— entitling you to win *th-reeee*—"

"Hold on a—"

"—newly minted di-ems!"

"Di-ems?" Rachel says, momentarily diverted.

"Di-ems, Ms. Cooper. Thir-ty cents! Now, Ms. Cooper, your first trivia question—take your ti-em, Ms. Cooper, this is not easy. Who, Ms. Cooper, who is buried in Grant's Tomb? Stumped? Ms.—"

"Who is this?"

"Ron Heartbroker of Station WTI—"

"Who is this?" she repeats.

"Lewis," he says meekly.

"Lewis Olswanger?"

"Wait a second, let me check . . . Yeah, this is Lewis Olswanger. Is this Rachel Cooper?"

"Wait a second, let me check."

"Hi, Rachel."

"Hello, Lewis."

Then there's a silence. Rachel thinks of things to say but dismisses most of them as uninteresting or silly. Finally, when she can't stand the silence any longer, she says, "So what are my other questions, Ron?"

"Ron?" Lewis says in his Lewis voice, sounding alarmed.

"Mr. Heartbroker, are you having problems?"

"Mr.—? Oh, yes, yes, yes, yesss, Ms. Cooper. Problems is my second—" He breaks off and yells away from the phone, "Okay! I hear you. Rachel? Sorry, my father wants the phone, and when he wants the phone—"

"Right. Bye, Lewis."

56

"Wait, Rachel! Uh . . . Ron Heartbroker wants to know if he made an ass of himself."

"Oh, no, he was just doing his job, wasn't he, Lewis?"

"Well, he's awfully . . . um . . . sensitive. So, are you sure?"

"I'm sure."

"Would you mind saying it again, just to reassure him?"

"Yes. I mean, no, I wouldn't mind."

"Say the whole thing," Lewis urges. "Like this: 'No, Ron Heartbroker did not make an ass of himself.'"

"You said it, I second it."

"You're not just saying it to be nice to me?"

"Yes, I am."

"Oh!"

"But I mean it, too."

"I hope so! Bye, Rachel."

"Bye, Lewis."

About ten minutes after they hang up, the phone rings again. "Mrs. Cooper," a brisk voice says, "this is Dr. North. I want you to come into my office tomorrow—"

"Dr. Lewis North, I presume," Rachel says coyly.

"Mrs. Cooper, this is Dr. Edward North, we need to talk about your father."

"Oh. Oh! Dr. North. I'm sorry, I didn't—I mean, this isn't—"

"I'll put Betty on and you can make an appointment with her."

There's a click. Then, "Mrs. Cooper? Betty, here. When would be a good time for you to come into the office? Dr. North only has morning hours tomorrow. How about ten o'clock? I have an opening then."

"This isn't—I mean, this is Rachel."

"Oh, I see I have a noon slot open, too, Mrs. Cooper. How about that?"

"Noon?" she says. "Twelve o'clock? That sounds okay."

"See you then, Mrs. Cooper."

"You'll see my mother," Rachel says in one last attempt to make matters clear, but Betty has already hung up.

Rachel sits down with a jam tart and a book, but she doesn't read. She's bothered that the doctor wants to talk to her mother about her grandfather. Why doesn't he talk to Izzy? Does he think because Izzy's in his eighties, he's incompetent or senile? The injustice of it annoys her, and some dim impulse to make up for this to her grandfather sends her to the phone.

"Yes?" her grandfather says.

"Grandpa, is that you?"

"Who'd you expect, President Reagan?"

"It's me," Rachel says. "Your granddaughter," she adds, to be perfectly clear.

"What do you want, Rachel?"

This stops her dead for a moment. Then she says, "You still have those pains in your stomach?"

"They went away."

"Oh, good. I'm all over the flu, too."

"Rachel, I'm playing Scrabble with my neighbor, Miller. Maybe you could let me get back to it?"

She barely puts down the phone when it rings again.

"This is Dr. Roof," a falsetto informs her. "I, Dr. Roofus Roof, am a well-known saxual expert throughout the world and universe. Dr. Roof solves all saxual problems. Maybe you got saxual problems you want solved? Tell Dr. Roofus Roof. Go ahead, please."

"Hi, Lewis," Rachel says.

"Yo, Rachel. What're you doing?"

"Well," Rachel says, "not much, except talking on the phone."

"Getting a lot of weird calls, are you?"

"You could say so."

"Say so," says Lewis.

"So," says Rachel.

"Say, I like a person who says so."

"I do, too."

"Excellent."

"We're in agreement," says Rachel.

"Verrrry good," says Dr. Roof. "That is a splendid start for a varm, luving relationship. Although, I must varn you, zere will certainly be a few little saxual problems . . ."

On the phone, Rachel decides, Lewis is like a different person. For one thing, he talks. For another, he's funny. And besides that, he has a deep, resonant voice, which she appreciates for the first time. "You have a nice voice," she says.

"I do?"

"Uh-huh."

"Nice how? Give me some of the details."

"Well, it's kind of deep."

"Any more?" he urges. "This is good for my ego."

"It's kind of deep—"

"You said that already."

"—and soothing."

"Soothing? Rachel, is this another way of saying *boring?* Do I put you to sleep, Rachel?"

"Maybe you should go into radio, Lewis. I think you have a radio voice."

"That's interesting. Radio instead of engineering, which is where my father wants me to go. What do you think, Rachel? Can you see me wearing a tie and sitting in an office with my computer and calculator?"

"You could be the other kind of engineer, the kind who works outdoors on roads and bridges and wears big, laced-up boots."

"And plaid shirts," Lewis says, his voice brightening. "The only thing, Rachel, I'd need shoulder pads in all those plaid shirts. You know, if you go out on one of those jobs and you have runty shoulders, they all just laugh at you."

"There you are, radio's perfect for you," Rachel says. "Nobody can see your shoulders on radio."

Rachel's half asleep when her parents come home, and in the morning, as usual, she's slow and not at her best. It's not until her father has gone to work and she and her mother are both on the way out of the house that she remembers Dr. North's call.

Shirley's hand flies to her chest. "He called? Why didn't you tell me last night?"

"Ma, I was sleeping. I'm telling you now."

"You should have told me right away. You should have left me a note."

"I'm sorry," she says. Why is her mother making such a fuss in such a loud voice? They are standing on the front steps, and across the street, Raymond Ramiro, who's in her class, is leaving his house. She's sure he's looking at them. She shifts her knapsack from one shoulder to the other.

"Why does he want to see me?" her mother says. "What's it about?"

"Something about Grandpa. That's all I know."

60

Rachel wants to leave but she can't. That note of anxiety ringing in her mother's voice holds her there as firmly as ropes.

"What is he going to tell me?" Shirley takes off her glasses and wipes them on her jacket sleeve. Her eyes look naked.

She is scared, Rachel thinks, and for a moment she resists, stubbornly, her mother's fears. They are not her fears. Then she says, "Ma. Do you want me to go to the doctor's with you?"

Her mother looks at her. "You?"

Rachel stiffens. Is it really that outlandish an idea? She went along to the hospital to pick up her grandfather, didn't she? Why is this any different? She only offered because her mother looked like she needed support. Rachel goes down the steps. "I'm going to school."

"Mouse," her mother says. Rachel turns. Her mother nods. "The doctor's on Collamer Street. Can you get a bus from school?"

TEN

Rachel's stomach rumbles. She's hungry. She hasn't eaten since morning. She's sitting next to her mother, facing Dr. North across his big cluttered desk. They've been here about ten minutes, and all that time Dr. North has been talking.

"You can see right here, Mrs. Cooper"—he swivels around in his chair—"this smudgy place and this one here." He points to two dark spots, one on each of the bluish X rays of Izzy's lungs pinned up behind his desk. "This is a nodule growing on the lining of the lung. This disease your father has is called mesothelioma. It typically attacks the lining of the lung and moves out from there. Now this other spot— you see it here?—it's in the lung itself."

Rachel's hand dips into her pocketbook, searching for a stray lemon drop or an old piece of chocolate. Nothing. Why didn't she think to buy a sandwich or a slice of pizza on the way over to the doctor's? *Stop thinking about your stomach,* she tells herself. *This is serious. What's the matter with you?*

She sits up straighter. She looks at Dr. North, watches his mouth forming words, hears the words, understands what the words mean, but somehow doesn't make sense of them: ". . . disease seems to be advancing . . . classic long period of hibernation . . ." He's talking about her grandfather. She thinks he's saying Izzy is going to die, but this is so unlikely—Izzy, that roaring, irritable man?—that she can't take it seriously. She can't even take Dr. North seriously. Today, with his shirt sleeves rolled up, he looks even more cherubic than the first time Rachel saw him, in the hospital. His headful of blond curls shines in the sunlight filtering through the venetian blinds. He just doesn't look like a doctor.

"This cancer is associated with people who have worked with asbestos. You might have heard of it as asbestosis," Dr. North is saying in his careful manner, pronouncing each syllable. As-bes-toe-sis. "Did your father ever work with asbestos?"

Shirley clasps and unclasps her pocketbook. "He was a stonemason. He worked outdoors mostly, walls, foundations. . . ."

"How about during the Second World War? Did he work in the shipyards? The literature indicates that this disease is showing up just now in a lot of those people."

"No shipyards."

"You're sure?"

"Yes, but he did work for a little while in a factory. I don't know what he did there, but it wasn't for very long. I think it was just four or five months."

Dr. North nods. "It doesn't take long for the damage to be done." He looks down at the file, which is open in front of him. "And he was a pretty heavy smoker back then. That makes people much more susceptible." He takes a prescription pad out of his desk. "I gave your father some pills for discomfort, you remember. I'll write you another prescription that you can use for him when—"

Shirley takes a long, loud breath. "When I took my father home from the hospital, you said he had a clean bill of health. I was right there. I heard you say it. A clean bill of health. Right, Rachey?" But she doesn't look at Rachel, only at the doctor. "And now you're telling me something else. You're telling me, you're saying he has a very bad disease and—"

"Mrs. Cooper." Dr. North leans across the desk. "I'm sorry. What I said in the hospital, I said for your father's benefit. He's an old man. I wanted to give him optimism. At that point, at any rate, I didn't have the lab results, I only had my suspicions. You remember when you brought him into my office the first time? I had a hunch right then, but of course, I couldn't be sure. Not without the lab tests."

"Yes," Shirley says, "the tests are important."

"You understand, though, even if I had had the test results when you got him from the hospital— even then I wouldn't have said anything to him. I wouldn't want to hit him in the face with something like that."

"No," Shirley says. "Who wants to tell someone something like that?"

Dr. North frowns. "Don't forget, we're not one hundred percent sure of the diagnosis. To be one hundred percent sure of what we have in your father's lungs, we would have to do a biopsy. We would have to do surgery, cut him open just to see what we have there. Do you want to do that?"

Shirley shakes her head. "No. No," she says.

"And, you know, with asbestosis there's nothing we can do, anyway."

"Chemotherapy?" Shirley says.

"Not a viable option. For a man his age it would just be experimental. Now, you're the closest relative, is that right?"

"Yes. My brother is in England. It's funny, just the other day I wrote him about Daddy's little stomachache and that sometimes he's a little short of breath." She sounds short of breath herself. "And I said, 'Well, Lenny'"—again she catches her breath—"'what can you expect when someone is eighty-three, but Daddy's going to go on for another twenty years.'"

Dr. North twirls his pen between his fingers. "Some people say, 'Tell the patient everything.' I don't agree. No."

As Dr. North talks, what Rachel hears above all else is the word *patient*. That single word enters her mind like a bore, drills down into some place where she has been—what? hiding from understanding as if behind a wall? Some people say, "Tell the patient everything." And what does the patient say? *The patient. The patient.* The wall crumbles, Izzy is there behind the wall, his lungs are there, those polluted lungs, and everything is clear; all the things Dr. North has been saying, all the convoluted explanations and long words now make simple sense. Her grandfather is going to die.

"I don't see what good it will do to tell your father the exact facts," Dr. North is saying. "Will that cure him? No way. It could even make things worse. It could very well depress him, take away his will to live. The body needs hope to fight its battles."

"Are you saying there's a chance?" Shirley says.

"There's always a chance. I'm not God. I only can tell you what I believe, based on my education and experience." Dr. North's eyes stray to Rachel. "I'm going to lay it on the line for you. My educated guess is that your father has two, maybe three months, at the most, to live."

Shirley is opening and closing the clasp on her pocketbook. For a moment the tiny, silver, clicking sound is the only sound to be heard in the office.

Rachel's eyes fix on the blue pictures of Izzy's lungs, the lungs that give him life. There, on those lungs, are the spots that will destroy his life. Life and death lying side by side, as close as two kittens in a litter.

Dr. North uncaps his pen and writes on a prescription pad. "I'm giving you twenty-one refills on this. I want Mr. Shapiro to be comfortable." He pushes back his chair. It's a sign for them to leave.

Rachel and her mother stand up. Is that it? Rachel thinks. Is that all? It seems to her that something is missing. "Dr. North," she blurts, "wait. What happens now?"

"What happens now?"

"You say my grandfather's so sick. Well, up to now, he just seems to be the way he always is. So what happens now?"

"What happens now," Dr. North says, "is that he will get weaker and weaker. That will be the chief sign. Weaker and weaker," he repeats.

ELEVEN

"Coach Al," Rachel says, flipping open her steno notebook, "can I start this interview with some background questions?"

"This is for the school paper, Rachel?" He's taking down the volleyball net. Except for the two of them, the gym is empty. Their voices echo.

"Yes, I'm doing a feature on some of the special teachers."

"I don't think I'm special," Coach Al says, but he looks pleased. He's short, stocky, with powerful-looking arms. He's wearing green pants, a green-and-white-striped shirt.

"Are you married, Coach Al?"

"Divorced."

"Do you have children?"

"My daughter. Kimberly. She lives with her mother."

He falls silent, and Rachel wonders if she's making him sad. She remembers seeing him one day last summer at the salad bar in the supermarket, filling a clear plastic container with chunks of tomatoes and carrots and mounds of potato salad. Her eyes sting unexpectedly with the recollection.

"Did you always want to be a coach?" she says.

"When I was growing up, all I wanted was to be a basketball player, Rachel."

"What happened? Was there a moment when things changed, when you knew you wanted to make coaching your life's work?" She wonders if she sounds okay.

This has been a strange day. Actually, *she's* been strange, here and not here, in and then out of herself—she doesn't know any other way to describe it. One moment she's in residence, telling herself she really has to work harder on learning geometry theorems; the next moment she's floating, up there on the ceiling, Rachel observing Rachel observing Rachel.

"Well, Rachel," Coach Al is saying, "I realized when I was about seventeen that I had stopped growing and I could never be a pro basketball player because I was too short. It wasn't a matter of heart. I had plenty of that. I was just too short to make it."

She thinks about giving up her own dream of being a writer. Why would it happen? Maybe if she lost her fingers? But then she could talk her stories into a tape recorder. What if she lost fingers and voice both? She read a book once about a man who was totally paralyzed. The only sounds he could make were grunts and gasps. But his toes had movement, so he learned to paint and type with his toes.

Coach Al is looking at her. She's not supposed to be daydreaming. She's supposed to be asking intelligent questions. She clears her throat. "How did you feel giving up your dream? Was it awful?"

Coach Al wraps the net around the post. "I was disappointed, but then I thought, well, it's not the end of the world. I went out for all the sports in college: basketball, baseball, wrestling. My coach told me, concentrate your abilities, Albert, always concentrate the abilities. Stick to one thing, you'll steadily improve, and it's going to give you confidence. Good advice. I went to wrestling. I became a good wrestler. I have quite a few trophies at home."

"Was there anything special you did?"

"Besides training hard? I'd always make sure to wear something green. Don't ask me why, just a little thing of mine. They started calling me the Green Flash. They put that in the college newspaper. The Green Flash wins again."

"Grn fish," Rachel writes, and she gets a green flash of her own. Coach Al is enjoying this interview. Maybe nobody ever asks him about himself. Everyone asks him questions all the time, but it's always: "Coach Al, can I get an excuse from gym?" "Coach Al, will you help me with my jump shots?" "Coach Al, will you show me that grip again?"

"Let me mention this friend of mine," Coach Al is saying. "Lefty Lefkowitz. Prime guy, great athlete, but he never neglected the books. Hit the books, Albert, he told me, you'll never be sorry. Now, that's more good advice. Are you putting that down?"

Rachel nods. She has been taking notes steadily, but when she looks down at the pad, what she sees are four scrawled words she didn't even know she had written: "My grndfthr is dyng."

"Coach Al." She breaks into the middle of a sentence. "My grandfather is dying." Her heart bumps in her chest and she looks down at the polished floor. She didn't know she was going to say that, and she doesn't know why she did say it.

Coach Al blinks. His eyes are baby blue. "I'm sorry, Rachel." He pats her arm.

Outside, it's raining, and she finds Helena waiting for her near the front door. Helena takes Rachel's arm. "That was a long interview. How's Coach Al?"

"Helena," Rachel says, "my grandfather is sick. He's dying."

"Oh, Rache, no." Helena puts her arm around Rachel, but all Rachel can think is that she's done it again. First Coach Al, now Helena. Isn't she just using Grandpa Izzy's illness to make herself important? Behind her ribs, there seems to be an empty space. Has she no feelings? She had tears for Coach Al's loneliness, but where are her tears for her grandfather?

My grandfather is dying. Does she plan to tell everybody? The man behind the counter when she buys a pack of gum? *My grandfather is dying.* Strangers on the street? *My grandfather is dying.* Maybe if she keeps saying it, she will feel it, she will believe it. In the movies, dying people clutch their chests, they fall *splaat* on the floor with a great gush of blood or ketchup, or they raise their heads for a last few brave words. What has that got to do with Izzy? "Foolish! I'll be here after you're gone, Shirley. . . . Rachel, maybe you'll let me go back to my game now." Are those the words of a dying man?

TWELVE

"How did the doctor look when he told your mother?" Helena says. She's toweling her hair dry. They both got wet on the way home. "Was it hard for him to say? Did he look upset, or just matter-of-fact, like he tells people bad news all the time? I'm not being morbid," she adds, throwing down the towel. "It's just I've never been in this situation and—"

"I know," Rachel says. She's sitting cross-legged on Helena's bed. "I understand. It's like research for an actress. Right? The doctor? Well, he looked something like an angel with a stomachache. He was kind of brisk, actually, like he wanted to get it over with—but not in a mean way," she adds.

"Like this?" Helena contorts her face. It's meant to be symbolic of Dr. North's feelings. Rachel wants to tell her it's good, she's got it, she's caught the essence of the doctor, but she can't.

"Helena, that's terrible, it's just acting, there's nothing real about it." Then, seeing Helena's disappointment, she says, "Maybe you just won't play heavy parts. You don't have to, you're so good at comedy. Remember Countess Natasha?" Last year, Helena played a fat, imperious Russian countess in a spoof the Theater Club put on. "All you had to do was give your daughter—what was her name,

71

Olga?" Helena nods. "Well, all you had to do was give her a look and everybody was falling off their chairs."

"Rachel, an actress needs to know a lot of stuff. It's like the thing Coach Al just told you. I'm trying to concentrate on different kinds of experiences. Anyway, I don't want to be just funny. That's too easy. Tell me about your mother, okay?"

"What about her?" Rachel gets up and starts fiddling with some of the little jars and pots on Helena's dressing table.

"You know . . . how did she look when he told her—" She breaks off. "I'm sorry, Rachel, this is ghoulish, isn't it?" She comes up behind Rachel and hugs her. "This whole thing was dumb of me. I was just thinking about acting. I forgot it was real for you and your mom."

"It's okay."

"Are you sure?"

Rachel nods. What she doesn't say is that with all her talk, it's still not real enough for her.

A few minutes later, the door bell rings. They go downstairs and it's Mikey, in a bright yellow slicker, with Lewis Olswanger, in a green rubber cape, lurking behind him.

"Well, hello," Helena says, in her best, bright voice.

Rachel gives her a look. Did Helena know these two were going to show up? Rachel's not sorry to see Lewis, but she hates the feeling of being thrown together with him. Besides, he looks unhappy and doesn't say anything, not even hello. So Rachel doesn't say anything either and they silently follow Mikey and Helena, who are chatting away already, into the kitchen. Maybe, Rachel thinks, she and

72

Lewis need telephone wires strung between them in order to talk.

Mikey's hungry, he just got off work, so Helena makes cheese sandwiches on English muffins. "How about you, Lewis?" He shakes his head. Helena and Rachel sit on the counter, dangling their legs. Mikey tips back in a chair. And Lewis stands near the door, looking either excruciatingly bored or ready to fall asleep.

Rachel takes Lewis's sleepiness personally. Lewis's smile at her at the theater? A reflex. The telephone calls? An aberration. All that funny stuff and sensitivity? Fake! So why is he here now? She knows the answer to that. Helena and Mikey cooked this up. Back to square one. Poor Rachel needs a boyfriend. Who will we get for poor Rachel? Et cetera, et cetera.

She concentrates on piling up little packets of Sweet 'N Low from a jar on the counter. She tops the packets with a spoon and then another spoon, balanced across the first one. Last week, Mr. Orso, the art teacher, gave an assembly. "Art is everywhere. Art is life. Life is art. Art is long and life is short. Look for art in everything."

"Art who?" Rachel whispered to Helena.

"A famous artist," said Mr. Orso, rising on his toes as he spoke, "was sitting and drinking one night with a friend—drinking coffee, so cut out the snickering down there in the third row, I know who you boys are—and dabbling around with the ashes in an ashtray. Ordinary cigarette ashes—are you listening out there, you might learn something—moving them this way and that. And when he got through, *just by dabbling with ashes,* he had made a work of art!"

Rachel has just made a Work of Art. The Leaning Tower of Sweet 'N Low. Or maybe, Sweet 'N Low with Two Spoons.

"Mikey is going to have his pilot's license by the time he graduates," Helena says.

"Mmm." Rachel nods and sneaks a look at Lewis. He's still dozing over there by the door.

"If I can't get a job with one of the major airlines, I'll get a job with one of the commuter services. I'll need to build up my experience hours."

"Bad idea," Rachel says. "Commuter services have four times as many accidents as the major airlines."

Mikey lets the chair legs down with a thump. "Oh, I don't think so."

"It doesn't matter what you think, Mikey. It's a fact."

There's a little silence. Rachel's cheeks start burning. She has just said something socially inept.

Helena covers for her, starts talking about the next production of the Theater Club. "There's this one scene where they're all sitting at the table, eating, and the guests are tiptoeing past them—"

Mikey gathers up the crumbs of his cheese sandwich. "Just don't volunteer to make the food for that scene, Helena. This is all she knows how to make," he says. "Toasted cheese on English muffins. Every time I come here, it's toasted cheese on English muffins."

"If you don't like it, Mikey," Rachel says, "why don't you make your own damn sandwiches?"

Lewis's head jerks up. He's definitely awake now.

Mikey is watching her. Probably wondering what's going to come out of her mouth next. Rachel wonders the same thing. "Next time, Rachel," Mikey says, "I'll take your advice."

"You'll make your own sandwich?" Helena says. "That's progress. Yaaa!"

Rachel hops off the counter. "Well, I guess I'll go." No one, she notices, begs her to stay.

Helena follows her to the front door. "Rache, you okay?"

Rachel nods. "I'll call you later."

Outside, she takes lots of deep breaths. It's still raining, a fine, cool drizzle. She raises her face, lets the rain cool her cheeks. Make your own damn sandwiches, Mikey. She doesn't know if she should laugh or cry. What an idiot she is, a total social idiot.

She's halfway down the street when she hears behind her the sound of wet, thudding footsteps. She turns and here comes Lewis, his green cape flying out behind him.

"Ms. Cooper, I presume," he says, panting to a stop.

So he's talking again, but Rachel is cautious. "Hi."

"It's raining," he says. "In case you didn't notice, I thought I'd point it out."

She nods her head in appreciation.

"I never asked you how you liked the *Pinafore*."

"I did."

"Yeah, it was great. First time I ever saw that. My Aunt Lucy couldn't go, so she gave me her ticket. Who were you with, your grandfather?"

"I was with my father."

"Oh, sorry, I thought—"

Everybody is apologizing to her today. "My *grandfather* is sick," Rachel says. "Terminal." Lewis stares at her, as if he doesn't understand. So Rachel says it once more. "My grandfather is dying." And this time, she doesn't know why, the words fall down inside her like stones.

75

THIRTEEN

Dear Jeremy,

It's late, nearly midnight, Ma and Daddy are sleeping, I've been reading, but I'm still not sleepy. I guess you know about Grandpa Izzy. Ma said she was going to call you and Phil, and anybody else in the family who ought to know, to tell you that he's pretty sick. I don't know why I said that. He's not "pretty sick," Jeremy, he's going to die. There. That makes about ten times I've said it, and you're the first person that there's a reason for saying it to.

You know what, Jeremy? When I was about ten years old, my favorite book was *Little Women*. I cried my way through it at least five times. Every time I read it, I cried buckets over Beth's dying. And now Grandpa's dying, and I haven't cried at all. Sometimes I really think something's wrong with me.

I think I'm going to stop and tear up this letter, because it's pretty stupid and I don't want you to despise me, and—

Dear Jeremy,

Do you know that I tell you things I wouldn't tell any other person in the world? This is true.

Who else is there? My friend Helena. Yes, I tell her things, but not everything. It's nothing to do with Helena, I don't think she would hate me or anything like that, it's more to do with me. I really can't bear the thought that anybody would know some of the things I think or do. Maybe I tell you stuff because you're so far away, and if you are shocked, I don't know it. I can't tell Ma or Daddy anything. They think of me as their sweet little daughter. To begin with, okay, I'm short, but *not little*. Know what I mean? And I'm not sweet, definitely not sweet. They've got me all wrong.

The other day when Ma had to go to the doctor's about Grandpa, I saw that she was really feeling scared about it, and I felt sorry and offered to go with her. You should have seen the look she gave me! So surprised. Practically dazed. A look like, *You? You would do something so grown-up?* As if going with her to Dr. N's was some kind of incredible feat of moral strength. That's the kind of thing about the parents that sometimes drives me berserko. But honestly, sometimes I can also be controlled and moderate and *très* mature. I hope you believe this! Especially after you hear what happened last night. After that, you probably won't believe I even *know* what moderation means.

Hey, Jeremy, am I totally demento to tell you these things about myself? I put all my terrible stuff, all my craziness, all my screams and fears and tantrums down on paper. I like doing that! I admit I like writing about it. And it really makes me feel better. But I'm also worried. Do you think I'm some kind of monster? Is that why you don't answer my letters? I'm not trying to make you feel

77

guilty (not much, ha ha), but it's getting through to me that if I want you to like me as much as I like you, I just might not be going about it the right—

Dear Jeremy, my brother confessor, how do you feel about all the things I'm always writing you? I guess it must be okay with you or you'd drop me a postcard with one of your usual to-the-point messages: "R. Cooper. Keep your troubles to yourself. I have enough of my own. Please find yourself another ear." Well, I guess until I do get the word, you are the one. You are chosen, Jeremy. So. Do you know about Grandpa? Has Ma told you yet? I was in the doctor's office with her and—oh! I just remembered something. I just remembered about you and Grandpa, the last time you were here, the things he said to you. So now I wonder how you feel about him being sick. Are you still mad at him? It seems like it's pretty awful to be mad at somebody who's dying. Shut up, Rachel, who are you to say anything? Sorry, Jeremy, I—

Dear Jeremy,

It seems I always write you when things are bothering me. So here goes again. Last night, Ma and I were in the kitchen. She was ironing, and I was memorizing geometry theorems. (I don't remember where Daddy was, maybe upstairs in the bathroom.) So, everything seemed fine, then Ma said, "My feet hurt." She was barefoot and wearing her old green bathrobe. (You know the one I mean? It's so old, you must remember it.) Anyway, I knew right away, just from the way she said her feet hurt, that she was feeling sort of down, so

78

I asked her if she soaked her feet when she got home from work. She said, "It's not just my feet. I have a backache, too. And I couldn't sleep all last night thinking about your Grandpa Izzy."

So I said, "Oh." And that's when everything started to go wrong.

Ma got right on my case. "Oh? Is that all you can say?" And then, Jeremy, she said, "I lost my mother, too."

I thought, Come on! That happened a million years ago. I didn't say it, but she must have guessed what I was thinking. Because, right away, her voice got sort of quivery and she said, "I never got over that. I loved my mother, and now I'm going to lose my father."

I know this doesn't make sense, but the way she said it, I felt as if she was saying I didn't love her. And right then, at that moment, she was right! I didn't! And the look she gave me, sort of sad and condemning at the same time, as if I'd done something really wrong, made me mad. So then I did do something wrong. I said, "Ma, look at it this way. Grandpa Izzy's never that nice to you, anyway." Jeremy, I shouldn't have said it! I mean, it is the truth, but why did I have to say it? And then I made it even worse, because I didn't shut up. I just kept going. "If you look at it logically—"

"Logically!" she said. "Oh, Rachel, you cold heart."

She said it—and it happened. I went cold. Cold all over. I swear my heart turned to ice, stopped beating, and before I knew what I was doing, I shoved the sugar bowl off the table, the English china one with the hand-painted daisies on it.

Jeremy! The minute I did it, I was sorry. I could

hardly breathe. I was ashamed. I was mad. I was hurt. I wanted to laugh, too! And my eyes were smarting. I didn't know all the things I felt, I didn't know why I did it. I wanted to undo it. I picked up the pieces and started putting them together. "I think I can glue it," I said.

And Ma was saying "My sugar bowl" in this teeny little voice, like she was on the verge of really bawling. "My sugar bowl." And every time she said it, I felt worse than ever. I kept thinking, *What kind of person am I?*

"My sugar bowl."

"I'll glue it together, I can do it, I can fix it, Ma."

"No. I don't care. Don't you understand anything?" And then she did start to cry! I wanted to do something to help her or stop her tears. Honestly, I did! Like hug her or something, but I was frozen, I couldn't move. And then I thought, *She hates me because I'm not crying like she is.* I knew she was crying about Grandpa, Jeremy! I knew it, I'm not totally stupid. And I wasn't crying. I haven't. I *can't.* He's my grandfather. He's going to die. I keep telling myself that. And I can't cry. Is it because part of me keeps telling the other part of me just what I said to Ma: Well, he's not that nice a person, anyway.

So there I was in the kitchen, thinking all this, and Ma is crying and I'm not doing anything, not saying, "I'm sorry, Ma," not hugging her, not making her feel any better. But finally, I sort of unfroze and I put my arms around her and gave her a little hug. And then! Then, Jeremy, I felt worse than ever because that was all I had to do. She gave me this really sad, sad, melting look and said, "Oh, baby, oh, Rachey . . ." And she held on to me and sort of sniffled sadly. When Daddy came downstairs, that was the way he found us.

Am I going to send this letter? I don't know. In case I do, much love from me, yr old sis, Rachel.

FOURTEEN

"Hi, Lewis." It's Thursday evening and Rachel is calling Lewis from work. "I'm standing in a telephone booth. I'm on my break at work."

"I didn't know you worked."

"Every Thursday, Lewis, from five o'clock to nine o'clock, you can see me at Martin's Big K Market putting groceries in bags and loyally wearing my red Martin's Big K Market T-shirt."

"If his name is Martin, why is it called the Big K?"

"Well, there are various theories. One is that it's for his daughter, whose name is Kathi. Another is that it just sounds better than Martin's Market."

"Okay, now why is your Martin's Big K Market T-shirt red?"

"Sometimes it's yellow. In either case, on the front it says, MARTIN'S BIG K MARKET IS OKAY. And on the back it says, PUT YOUR PART TIME TO WORK AT MARTIN'S BIG K."

"Does that make sense?"

"I don't think that matters to my boss. When I first got the job, I had to wear a badge that said, I'M NEW AND I THANK YOU FOR CARING."

"For caring?"

"My boss likes that word. Leah, this woman who's worked here for a thousand years, says whenever she goes in to ask for a raise, he tells her he cares. She says, 'Thank you, I need more money.' And he says, 'I wish I could help you. I care!' And then he tells her what a hard time he's having at home. She says she always ends up comforting him and getting about half the money she wants."

"So the phone booth is your hangout on your break?"

"Don't knock it. This booth is about twice as big as the employees' lounge and three times as clean."

"Tell me how long your break is, Rachel. I was just going out to the store for my mom."

"Can you spare ten minutes?"

"For you? At least eight."

"If you come over here to shop, Lewis, I'll be your bag girl."

"Is that a threat?"

"Pardon me?"

"Well . . . I don't know, Rachel, you might want to put a bag over my head."

"You have a bizarre mind."

"That's true," Lewis admits with a modest snicker.

"Lewis, I give you my word, I will never bag your head."

So things are progressing, at least with Lewis. In the Cooper house, there's a sadness, a heaviness in the air. Rachel's mother sits at the supper table and stares blankly down at her plate. Or she sighs deeply and repeatedly, as if she can't get enough air. Then Rachel knows that her mother is thinking about Grandpa Izzy. Which Rachel is not doing. She finds her own mind sliding away from thoughts of him. Slipping and sliding away from sickness thoughts and death thoughts to Lewis thoughts.

One of her favorite Lewis thoughts is to imagine

what kissing him would be like. Will be like. Because, if all this is leading anywhere, surely it's leading up to the coveted kiss?

On Saturday, they go to a movie together. It's almost a date but not quite. They each pay for their own tickets. Rachel buys the popcorn, Lewis buys the soda. They sit shoulder-to-shoulder. And they hold hands.

Of course, they're both looking straight at the screen, completely absorbed. It's a foreign film and they agreed, before they went, that they had heard so much about it, they had to see it. So now they are paying attention. They can't help it if their hands are uninterested in the movie's important message. They can't help it if their hands are doing this and that, if their fingers are nuzzling, linking and unlinking. They, themselves, are raptly attentive to the screen.

Rachel develops an itch on her nose. What a place for an itch. She wriggles her nose, but the itch remains. She frees her hand and scratches. Lewis's hand, now also free, having nothing to do, goes up to pull his ear and from there, ever so casually, drops down to clasp Rachel's shoulders. Rachel moves closer to Lewis, their heads meet and touch, and that's how they watch the rest of the movie.

Afterward they stop for hamburgers and talk nonstop. It's amazing, considering that the beginning of this friendship was almost totally silent, but they don't seem to run out of things to say to each other. They go from the movie to books, to Helena and Mikey, to their parents, teachers, school, the future, and back to the movie. They stay so long, they have to order more food, which is no problem, since Lewis says he's always hungry.

As they're finally getting ready to leave, Rachel is

thinking about that first day in the library. "Lewis, did you ever think we'd actually get to be friends?"

A thoughtful look comes over Lewis's face. "Friendship," he murmurs, draping his scarf around his neck, "is like pain. Explaining it is impossible."

Rachel sits down again. "Lewis. Did you just make that up? How did you do that? Even if I want to, I can never think of things like that."

Lewis's face brightens with what Rachel imagines to be a humble blush. "Aaaggh, Rachel," he says. "Even if I want to, I cannot tell a lie. I didn't think of that just now. I was waiting for a chance to say it. I came out tonight with it all prepared." He puts his head down on his arms. "Mercy on a poor sinner. It's worse than that. I didn't think that up. I—" He peers up at her. "I—"

"Borrowed it?" Rachel fills in helpfully.

"You're too kind. I stole it."

"Lewis, I always write down things I read or hear."

"Yes, but you don't memorize them to pass off as your own, so you can impress other people. Do you?"

"Uh . . . no."

"You must think I'm a goof."

"Uh . . . no."

"Are you sure?"

"Yes."

"Well, I think I'm a goof."

"You confessed," Rachel says. "It's not such a big crime." She wants to say something else compassionate and wise, but she doesn't get the chance, because Lewis leans across the table, over the ketchup and mustard, and rubs his nose against hers. And that, as any fool knows, is an Eskimo kiss.

FIFTEEN

"Here're your house keys, Ma," Rachel says on Sunday morning.

Shirley looks at her blankly. "I don't know if I can do this," she says to Rachel's father.

"Shirl, sure you can. Come on now." Manny straightens the back of her pink shirt.

"I don't know, I don't know. Going there as if everything is just the same, when it isn't, and—" She breaks off. "Where'd you find the keys, Rachel?"

"In the bathroom, on the shelf."

"I don't know what's the matter with me. I looked everywhere for them. I looked in the bathroom, I didn't see them." She stares at herself in the little mirror over the telephone table. "I look like something the cat dragged in. I don't think I've slept one good night this week. Not since the doctor told me."

"Remember what the doctor said, Shirl." Manny's voice is deep, calm. "He's not one hundred percent sure. You always hear about these cases where people confound the doctors. Maybe Izzy's one of them and he'll live to be a hundred and six."

"No." Shirley's eyes redden. "Dr. North said three months at the most."

Rachel thinks that her father is looking at the hopeful side. Her mother is looking at the bleak side. And what side is she looking at?

"Izzy looks too good to die," Rachel's father says.

"I know, it's so hard to believe."

"The thing, now, is to be just like always with him. Let him live and be well as long as possible."

Later, standing outside Izzy's door, they all hesitate. Then Manny knocks. "Hi, Dad," he calls, "it's us."

The door opens. "Come in, come in," the dying man says impatiently.

Even now, almost a week after the death sentence, he looks the same as always. He sounds the same as always. He acts the same as always. "Shirley, put down those bags. . . . Sit down, Rachel, don't fidget. . . . Did you bring me the newspaper, Manny?" And he sits down himself, hands flat on his thighs.

Again the whole day is as it always is. Rachel and Shirley cook a big meal. Manny eats everything with enjoyment. Izzy finds something to criticize. "I thought you were going to bring a rye bread." And when Manny brings out a bottle of wine, "What's the big occasion?"

Manny pours wine into three juice glasses. "I just got an impulse."

Izzy picks up his glass. "Is that so? Well . . . l'chayim." To life.

"L'chayim," Manny says, touching his glass to Izzy's.

"L'chayim," Shirley says. The glasses clink. Outside, it's begun to rain.

Later they turn on the TV, open the Sunday newspaper, get out the Scrabble set. It's a Sunday like any Sunday, like dozens of other Sundays, except that now Manny, Shirley, and Rachel share a secret—Izzy is dying. It's his life, his death, but he'll be the last one to know.

SIXTEEN

Rachel is home alone after school when the phone rings and a strange voice says, "Cooper residence? This is Alice Farnum. I live at 7587 Schuyler Hill and I have your father here. Mr. Shapiro. He fell down in the street outside my house. Can someone come get him?"

"I'll call my father," Rachel says.

"Who is this?"

"This is Rachel. I'm the granddaughter. I'll call my father," she says again.

She dials Manny's office. The moment the phone is picked up and she hears her father saying, "Hello. This is Manny Cooper—" she starts talking. "Dad," she says urgently, "something's happened to Grandpa and I need your help—"

"— of MC Services," her father's disembodied voice continues. "I'm with a client at the moment, but if you'll leave your name and number—"

"—right away," Rachel finishes lamely, and waits for the buzz on the answering machine so she can repeat her message. "Dad," she finishes, "call me right back."

As soon as she hangs up, she realizes Manny might or might not be with a client. She remembers from last summer that he always popped on the machine when he left the office, whether it was for five minutes or fifty or the rest of the day. She considers calling her mother. Shirley would come running. But how? On her two tired feet? If she takes a bus from downtown where she works, she won't be here for at least an hour.

No, first she'd better call Alice Farnum back and tell her someone's coming, but it might be a while. She picks up the phone and puts it down again. Why didn't she get Alice Farnum's phone number? How dumb. She looks up Farnum in the phone book. No Alice Farnum. No A. Farnum. Maybe it's spelled Farn*am*. Or Farn*em*. No. Farn*ham?* No. Maybe she heard wrong, and it's Farnsworth. Or Farnley. There's an A. J. Farnley (Alice Jane?) who lives on Seventh North. But no Farnums or Farnsworths or Farnhams on Schuyler Hill.

She calls her father again. "Hello. This is Manny Cooper of MC Services—" She hangs up. *Okay, don't panic. You'll go there, yourself.* She rummages through her parents' desk in the living room for a city map. Schuyler Hill sounds vaguely familiar, but she's not absolutely sure of the location. She finds old check registers, receipts, tax records, bills, photographs, and finally, almost lost among a stack of *National Geographic* maps, a city map. She opens it, smooths out the creases.

From where Izzy lives, Schuyler Hill doesn't look like more than another half mile or so. She can easily get there in twenty minutes, faster on foot than Manny, bucking downtown traffic, could make it in the car.

She runs out of the house, runs most of the way. She's so intent on being Rachel the rescuer that she hardly even notices the strange dogs that come barking out at her. And she's walking up Schuyler Hill, checking her watch (she made it in under twenty minutes), before it occurs to her that she's here but she's still got problems. If her grandfather is sick, what's she going to do with him?

Number 7587 Schuyler Hill is a small, bright yellow house with a lighted Christmas wreath hanging above the door. A woman with flaming red hair answers Rachel's ring. She is wearing silver slippers, a purple leotard, and a long purple skirt, slit up one side. Tiny, sparkling silver dots are sprinkled across her cheeks. She is perhaps forty years old and at least six feet tall. "Hello?" she says.

Rachel looks up in awe at this splendid apparition. "Mrs.—Ms. Farnum? I've come for my grandfather, Mr. Shapiro—"

"Are you Rachel? I thought your father was coming."

"I couldn't get in touch with him. I left a message."

Rachel follows Alice Farnum into the house, directly into a large, almost bare white room lined with mirrors. Her grandfather is sitting back on a small velvet couch, his eyes closed. There is a plaid blanket over his legs.

"Grandpa?" Rachel bends over Izzy. It's frightening how gray he looks.

His eyes open. "Where's Manny?"

"He couldn't come. How—"

"Don't ask me how I feel, Rachel. I feel like a fool." His breath is pumping hard. "Don't ask me how I fell. I don't know."

"Please, sit down." Alice Farnum indicates a pair of wooden folding chairs. Rachel takes one, Alice Farnum takes the other and crosses splendid legs. "Anybody could fall," she says consolingly to Izzy. She turns to Rachel. "An amazing thing happened. I was dancing, and when I dance, the spirits take me

90

over. I see nothing, I hear nothing, I feel nothing but the spirit of the dance." She flings back her head, her eyes close. Rachel stares in helpless fascination.

"Then something called to me. A voice called to me. I heard it very clearly. A voice saying, 'Help.'" She opens her eyes, holds out her arms. "Goose bumps rose on my flesh. I danced past the window, I looked out, and there he was, lying on the sidewalk!" She takes a deep breath, smiles at Izzy. "I didn't know what to think, I just ran out. I thought he was unconscious, but no, his eyes were open and his mind was as clear as a bell."

Rachel looks at her grandfather. He's nodding, and there's a tiny smile in the corners of his lips.

"I could see right away what kind of man your grandfather is," Alice Farnum goes on, in a more ordinary tone of voice. "I helped him up. I wanted to call an ambulance. 'No, no ambulance.' Isn't that what you said, Mr. Shapiro? You weren't even going to come inside my house. I had to plead with you. Such a stubborn man," she says, as if she's pinning a medal on Izzy.

Under the light of Alice Farnum's eyes, a little color has come back into Izzy's face and he sits up straighter. "You know how many years I've been walking up this hill?" he says to her. "And never had trouble?" He presses a hand over his chest and breathes heavily. "All of a sudden I lost my breath."

Rachel watches him. Is it happening to him again? His breath is short, shallow, but maybe he's just upset.

"I couldn't get my breath, and before I knew it . . . I was down, I was lying on the sidewalk . . . like a turtle on its back. In all my years, all the jobs I did . . ." He pauses for breath. "I never fell. When I was working, I used to run with the wheelbarrow full of bricks or cement. I never walked"—another pause—"anywhere. I had too much . . . too much energy for that. I ran up the ladders."

"I believe you." Alice Farnum smiles, and the silver dots on her cheeks dance.

"Now I don't run wheelbarrows, but I walk," Izzy says breathily. "Four miles a day." He presses a finger to the side of his nose. "Not so bad . . . for an old man . . . is it?"

Rachel looks at her grandfather in astonishment. Unless she's very mistaken, Izzy is flirting.

A dog shambles into the studio, an old mutt, the kind of dog Rachel feels rather kindly toward. Too old to bite, too tired to bark. He has floppy ears and some kind of growth on his lips. He lies down, panting, at Alice's feet, as if he's arrived after a long and difficult journey.

"My old darling." Alice takes the dog's face between her hands and kisses him. "This is Theo," she says.

"Hello, Theo," Rachel says. Theo raises his head and looks at her.

"He likes you," Alice says.

Izzy sinks back against the red couch. "I used to have . . . dogs."

"I knew you were a dog person," Alice says, getting up. "I can always tell." She goes into the kitchen. "You are a dog person, too, Rachel," she calls. "Aren't you?"

"Well," Rachel says. She likes Alice Farnum and doesn't feel like disillusioning her. "I guess you could say that."

Alice brings back a tray with a chunk of yellow cheese and a bowl of crackers and sets it down on a little table. "Let's have some food and see what we're going to do here," Alice says "Mr. Shapiro?" She holds out the tray. "I think we should call a taxi, don't you?"

"No," Izzy says. "I never take taxis. I'm not starting now."

"Maybe I should call my father again," Rachel says.

Alice gestures toward the kitchen. "The phone's right in there."

"Oh, I couldn't find you in the phone book," Rachel says.

"I'm unlisted."

"Hello," Rachel hears in one ear, "this is Manny Cooper of MC Services. I'm with a client right now . . ." And in the other ear, she hears Izzy saying, "I told you, I'm not taking a taxi home."

"Grandpa." Rachel sits down opposite him. "It's really a good idea. I can't get Daddy. He's out of the office."

"There's no . . . problem."

"I wish my car wasn't in the garage," Alice says.

"Nothing to talk about." Izzy stands up. "I'll go home . . . the same way I got here."

"You're not going to walk?" Alice says.

"Grandpa," Rachel starts, but Izzy brushes her away, just the way he's brushing the cracker crumbs off his fingers. Then he turns to Alice. "You're a fine woman. Thank you . . . for all your help." He walks to the door, opens it, and leaves.

Alice Farnum looks stunned. Rachel has just time to think that if Alice knew Izzy a bit better, she wouldn't be so surprised. Then Rachel runs after him, calling to Alice over her shoulder, "Sorry, I better go, thank you. . . ."

Izzy is already making his way carefully down the walk.

"Grandpa, wait for me." She catches up with him and takes his arm. "I'm going with you."

He frowns. "Go home," he says in his familiar, dismissive way. "Who needs you?"

Rachel bites her lip not to say, *You do. You were lying in the street an hour ago. You're dying.* It scares her how close she comes to saying it. Her face flushes. "I'm going back with you, Grandpa. Please don't argue with me."

Izzy breathes heavily. "I don't need you."

"Okay, I'm not doing it for you," she says. "If I didn't walk home with you, Ma would kill me."

"If you want to . . . waste your time."

"I do."

"I suppose . . . I can't stop you."

"No, you can't." For once, she has the last word with him.

SEVENTEEN

It's dark and chilly when Rachel finally gets home. The table is set for one, her father is reading the evening paper, her mother is washing dishes. "Why so late?" her mother says. "We ate already. Where were you?"

"Didn't you get my message?" she says to her father, but it's her mother who looks around, her eyes enlarged behind her glasses. "Message?" she says quickly. "What happened?" Her instincts for calamity are stronger than Manny's.

"Ma, don't get upset. Grandpa fell."

"He fell? What do you mean, he fell?"

"Fell," Rachel says. Her father has put down his newspaper; her mother sits down at the table. "He fell down on the sidewalk."

"Fell down on the *sidewalk?* Where is he?"

"Ma, listen, he's all right now."

"Where is he?"

"He's home, and—"

"Tell me from the beginning."

"I got this phone call—"

"Who called you?"

"When was this?" Manny says.

"A woman called me. Right after I got home from school. I had just walked in the house and the phone rang. It was Alice Farnum—"

95

"Who? Alice Farnum? Who's she? Is she somebody who lives in Grandpa's building?"

They can't wait for her to finish a sentence without interrupting. He was lying in the street? Did she mean the street or the sidewalk? Why didn't she call the ambulance? He must have hurt himself, falling that way. How did he look? He walked all the way home? *All the way home?* Why didn't she call a taxi? How could she let him walk home?

"I wanted to call a taxi, Ma. Anyway, you don't *let* Grandpa do things. He does them."

Her mother puts a plate of food in front of Rachel. "Go ahead, eat. Now tell me again, the whole story, from start to finish." And Rachel does. "At his building you went up in the elevator with him? You went in the apartment? And then what?"

"Then, nothing, Ma." Rachel picks at her food, but she has no appetite. Her stomach is too tense. "Grandpa said he'd just go to bed a little earlier and get some extra sleep. I tried to stay, but he kept telling me to leave. He insisted."

"How did he look?" her mother says for at least the fourth time. "Was he pale? Manny—do you think I should call him right now? No, what if he's sleeping? I better not disturb him."

The phone rings and Rachel scrapes back her chair. "Wait," Shirley says. "Don't answer. It's going to be bad news."

"Ma, it's probably Helena." Rachel's heart is pounding unpleasantly. What if it is bad news? Did she leave her grandfather too soon? If you fall down once, why not twice? She picks up the phone. "Hello?"

"Is Hazel there?" a man says.

The closeness to Helena's name momentarily confuses her. "Who?" she says. It's a mistake. Her mother is watching her with that frightened expression.

"Hazel," the man says.

"No, I'm sorry, you've got the wrong number."

"What? Where's Hazel?"

"Who is it?" her mother says. "What do they want?"

"Are you sure? Hazel Emworth," he repeats. "This is the number I was given."

"No, it's wrong. Better try again." She hangs up.

The phone rings again, almost at once. Her mother gasps. "This time, I know—" But it's the same man, still asking for Hazel.

"No," Rachel says distinctly. "No Hazel here. Don't call again," she adds. She sits down and tries to eat her supper. "If the phone rings, don't answer, Ma."

"We should call the doctor," her father says. "He should know about Izzy."

Her mother nods. "Manny, you do it, though. I can't talk to him now. I'm too nervous."

Manny gets Dr. North's answering service. "Everybody's on machines," he complains.

"Tell me about it, Daddy," Rachel says.

"Now I'm worried he won't call back until tomorrow," her mother says.

"Even if he doesn't, what could happen?" her father says.

"I don't know. I'm just worried." She looks at Rachel. "Aren't you going to eat any more than that?"

Later, when Dr. North calls back, Manny answers and starts to tell him about Izzy. Then he hands the phone to Rachel. "My daughter can tell you better what happened."

Dr. North listens without comment until she is

done. "I'm sorry to hear that," he says. "You say he didn't hurt himself?"

"I don't think so. He walked all the way home."

"That's good that he could do that."

"I wanted . . . this woman that took him in and I wanted to call a taxi, but he wouldn't let us."

"No, that's fine that he walked. As long as he could manage, why not?"

"It's just I thought he shouldn't—"

Her mother is standing right next to Rachel. "What is he saying, Mouse?"

"We want him to do whatever he can do, as long as he can do it," Dr. North says.

"Ask him if it's going to happen again," Shirley says.

"But things may be progressing faster than I originally thought they would. The tumors are pressing on his lungs. He's going to have less and less—"

"Sweetheart, ask him if there's anything special we should do for Grandpa."

Rachel covers the mouthpiece of the phone. "Ma!"

"What did I do? What did I say?"

"—oxygen available, and we may see other episodes."

"You mean he fell because he just—he couldn't get enough air?"

"That's correct. Putting it simply, yes. Yes, he fell because he ran out of air."

In school the next day, Rachel manages not to think about her grandfather very much. Maybe it's a reaction to the previous day, to all that tension. Or maybe, she thinks, when she remembers to think about Izzy, you just can't go around feeling miserable about someone else all the time, especially when you, yourself, are feeling just fine. The truth is, she has a good time and enjoys herself in school all day, especially in sixth-period study hall.

A spitball hits her on the side of her cheek. She turns around to see Lewis, two aisles away, staring innocently at her.

She picks up the spitball, raises her eyebrows. *Did you do this?*

Lewis holds up his hands in horror. *Would I do a thing like that? Would I throw a spitball?*

Rachel smirks. *Of course not.*

Lewis's eyebrows narrow and he points accusingly at Rachel. *You are the one who's done something . . . bad!*

She jabs her finger against her chest. Her face opens wide in surprise. *What did I do?*

Lewis points. *You know.*

Rachel taps her forehead, frowns sincerely. *Honestly, I have no idea.*

Lewis looks away, his arms folded.

Is he through playing the game? Rachel clears her throat. "A-hem," she says discreetly.

Lewis doesn't seem to hear her.

"A-hem!" She watches him closely. His left nostril curls contemptuously. She clears her throat rather loudly. *"A-hem."*

Mr. Esparza, who is the study-hall monitor, looks up from his book. "Please," he says in a pained voice. As usual, he's wearing cool ice-cream colors, a white suit, a pale blue shirt, a pale lavender tie.

Rachel writes Lewis a note on a scrap of paper. She folds the note, checks out Mr. Esparza—he's reading again—takes aim, and throws. The note lands just short of Lewis's desk.

He picks it up, takes his time unfolding it. Rachel watches him as he reads it. She wrote, "L., what's going on? What is this all about? Signed, Alarmed! Distressed! And oh so Puzzled." He looks over at her and she beckons. *Come on over here.*

Lewis's nose twitches. *Should I? Why?*

Rachel smiles coaxingly. *Because I want you to.*

Lewis slouches to his feet, crosses the space between their desks, and perches on the edge of her seat. "So what's the matter?" Rachel whispers.

"Nothing," he whispers back.

"Nothing?" she says loudly.

"Miss Cooper," Mr. Esparza says, "please. Mr. Olswanger, are you two studying?"

"Uh, yeah," Lewis says. His ears are red.

"Well, finish up, please."

"If it was nothing," Rachel whispers, opening one of her textbooks, "what was it all about?"

"I was just amusing myself," Lewis whispers back. "And you."

"Uuuck! You are a clown. A weird boy."

He nudges her. She nudges him back. Mr. Esparza looks up. "I have a feeling this is goodbye," Lewis says. He fishes a hard candy out of his pocket and gives it to Rachel. Then he goes back to his seat.

It's not until she gets home from school that Rachel even thinks of her grandfather. Then, just walking into the house brings the whole thing back. The phone in the hall looks ready to ring with bad news. Her mother's sweater, draped over a kitchen chair, seems to look at her reproachfully. *Didn't give him a thought all day, did you?* Even the refrigerator reminds her of Izzy when she takes out the salami wrapped in its little waxy stocking. Is her mother saving it for Sunday? Her grandfather adores salami. So does she, and she's been looking forward to a fried salami sandwich with plenty of mustard.

She puts the salami on the cutting board, takes a knife, and then just stands there, feeling guilty. Sighing, she returns it to the refrigerator. Nothing else looks quite as good. She settles for old, reliable peanut butter. While she eats, she leafs through the afternoon paper. She finishes the sandwich before the newspaper but continues reading. Then Helena calls and they talk, and it's all so nice and normal and ordinary. No tension, no guilt, no knots in her stomach.

Helena doesn't ask anything about Izzy, and why should she? It's Rachel who ought to be thinking about him, worrying about him, who ought, at the very least, to be calling him up to ask how he is, how he feels, if he's had any aftereffects from his fall. And it's Rachel who's managed to let a whole hour slip past since she came home from school, without doing any of those things.

As soon as she hangs up with Helena, she dials Izzy's number. The phone rings for a long time, longer than usual, long enough for Rachel to imagine Izzy lying alone and helpless on the floor.

He finally answers. "Yes? Who is it?"

"Grandpa, why didn't you answer the phone? Where were you?"

"Where do you think I was?"

"I don't know. The phone rang a long time."

"Rachel, when you're my age . . . it sometimes takes a while to do your business."

"Oh," she says. Izzy knows how to deflate her. "Well," she says after a moment, "how are you feeling today?"

"How should I feel?"

The words are the same as always, but she hears something else in his voice, some little quaver she's not used to hearing. "After yesterday, Grandpa, you could be excused for feeling a little tired. Did you stay in bed today and rest?"

"I did not."

"Oh. Did you go out?"

"I was downstairs in the lobby for a little while."

"I'll tell Ma."

"I've already talked to your mother today."

"She called you?"

"Mmm-huh."

"Grandpa, I was wondering, did you bruise yourself when you fell?"

Suddenly Izzy laughs. "I'm a big mess. My behind—excuse me—it's black and blue. My legs, too. I look like I've been in a big fight."

"Did you tell Ma that?"

"You think these are the first bruises I've ever had?"

"I guess not."

"I've been in plenty of fights in my life, Rachel. I've had black eyes, swollen lips, puffed-up ears."

"You make it sound like you were a boxer."

"A boxer and a wrestler and an all-around knocker. I grew up . . . in a rough world." She can hear him breathing over the phone. He speaks slowly, pausing often for breath. "You took care of yourself . . . or someone took care of *you*. You get my . . . meaning? You didn't walk through that world . . . with your eyes half shut, Rachel. You looked both ways and not . . . just at the corners." Another pause for breath. "Today, people complain, they say oh! . . . the good old days! but they . . . don't know. They don't know they got it good today."

When she hangs up a few minutes later, it occurs to Rachel that she just had a real conversation with her grandfather.

EIGHTEEN

"I spoke to my father today," Rachel's mother says at supper. "That fall took something out of him. I could hear it in his voice. He doesn't know how sick he is, but . . ." Her voice falters. "We were just lucky this time. What happens the next time?"

"It might not happen again," Manny says. "The doctor didn't say it would happen positively."

"It's going to happen again," Shirley says. "Maybe not tomorrow, maybe not even next week, but you know what the doctor said. Daddy's going to have less and less air. Get weaker and weaker. And you know him, he won't stay in, he won't give up anything. He's not saying, 'Okay, Shirley, I'm going to be careful.' Instead, it's some nonsense about Schuyler Hill—"

"That's where Alice Farnum lives," Rachel says.

"Oh, well, wonderful. He's going to walk up that hill? The man is sick, he can hardly speak a whole sentence without gasping, and he's going to walk up this big hill."

"Maybe he will," Manny says. "He's a determined man."

"Yes, and maybe he'll fall before he ever gets there. He doesn't have to walk up a hill to fall. He could fall outside, or in his apartment, or in the elevator. It could happen anywhere. It could happen anytime." What she wants to do, she says, is bring Izzy into their house to live, so they can watch over him. "He can sleep in the spare room. Manny, what do you think?"

Rachel's father nods. "I think we should do it. It'll give you peace of mind."

Rachel tries to imagine Izzy sleeping on one of the twin beds. She tries to imagine him eating breakfast with them and being here when she comes home from school. In the evening he will sit in Manny's green plaid chair facing the TV. He will deliver his opinions in his gravelly voice. He will be with them every day, every night, all the time. Then she remembers: *all the time* means a month, two months; at the most, three.

Rachel's mother pushes her chair away from the table. "I'm going to call Daddy right now." On the phone, she says in a fast voice, "Daddy, hello, I have something to talk to you about. Manny and I have decided we want you to come stay with us while—"

She gets no farther. No father, either. When she hangs up, she says with unaccustomed sharpness, "He's not sick, he's just a little short of breath. What am I making such a big fuss about? Is that the first time I ever heard of someone falling? I always make fusses, and even if he did fall again—which he is not going to do—what good can we do him when we're at work?"

"He's got a point there," Rachel's father says. "Anyway, you know what an independent man he is, Shirl. We don't want to take that away from him."

"I know, I know all that! It's wonderful that he's so independent, but right now I want him here. I can't go through every day at work with my heart in my mouth, thinking about my father falling down in the street somewhere."

"Let me try him," Manny says, and he gets up and phones Izzy. But he doesn't do any better than Shirley. "I'm sorry, sweetheart."

Shirley's face falls. "What am I supposed to do now?"

"I could try Grandpa," Rachel says.

Her parents look at her. "What would you say?" her mother says.

Rachel shrugs. "I don't know. It's just—you tried him, Daddy tried him. Why not me?" She's only about twenty percent serious. The whole thing with everyone pleading with Izzy is like a contest, she thinks. Just the sort of thing Izzy enjoys. Here he is sick, dying, and he's still got the upper hand.

"I don't know what good it will do, Rachey," her father says.

"I don't, either. It was just an idea." Silly idea. She has no influence with her grandfather.

"No, try," her mother says urgently. "Try. What can we lose?"

So she calls her grandfather and he says, "You, too? Now what? Don't you people have anything else to do but call me?"

Rachel plays for time. "Are you going for a walk tomorrow?"

"I always go for a walk, Rachel."

"Where are you going to go?"

"Rachel, why did you call me?"

"Well, Grandpa," she says, and then she's inspired. "I'll be over after school tomorrow. Wait for me. Wait until I come, for your walk."

"Wait?" he says, as if he's never heard anything so absurd.

105

"I'm going on your walk with you."

"Who invited you?"

"Me. I invited me." Before he can protest, she adds, "I'll say good-bye now." And, like a junior Izzy, she hangs up first.

Rachel raps on the door. "It's me, Grandpa. Rachel."

"Come in." He's sitting at the table by the window, with a bowl of soup. The TV is on, and he's watching an interview show as he eats. He nods briefly to her.

"Is that some of Ma's soup?" she says, just to be polite. He doesn't bother answering. She stands awkwardly in the middle of the room. Behind the table, the sun brightens, then fades. Rachel takes off her jacket, sits down on the couch. It occurs to her that if she has ever been alone with her grandfather before, she has no memory of it.

Her grandfather carries his bowl to the sink. He puts on a sweater, a windbreaker, a plaid cap, looks at her, and says, "This is your mother's idea, sending you over here."

"No, it wasn't. It was my idea." She follows him out the door, down the hall with its smells of frying meat and ironed clothes. From behind doors come the sounds of radios and kids crying. "Did you go out yet today, Grandpa?"

"I did not." He gives her a baleful glance. "I was ordered to wait."

She opens her mouth, closes it. No surprise that her grandfather isn't taking kindly to being bullied. Isn't that what she did? Bullied him? *I'm coming over. You wait for me.*

They go down in the elevator, out through the bare little lobby. They walk slowly toward Emerson

Avenue. He walks with his head a little thrust forward, looking neither to the right nor to the left. She adjusts her pace to his. Izzy says nothing. Neither does Rachel. There are not many people in the streets. A few kids on bikes. Runners. A woman with a bag of groceries in one arm, a child dangling from the other.

"Grandpa," Rachel says, when she can't stand the silence another moment, "what did you think when I said that I was coming over?"

"What did I think? I thought you were coming over."

It's so hard to talk to him. She tries again. "Well, I never said anything like that before. It must have surprised you."

"It didn't."

"It didn't surprise you?" That surprises her.

"Figure it out. You're . . . supposed to be smart."

"I know you didn't wait for me because you love my company," she says with an awkward laugh.

"Okay."

Is he agreeing with her? Why should that bother her? She knows what she said is true. He doesn't love her company—and she doesn't love his. So, they're even, and they'll both be relieved when today is over.

They pass Schuyler Hill. Izzy looks up, keeps walking. She hears his breath making a tiny wheezing sound in his chest with every intake of air. They walk past little houses with bikes in the front yards, the Greek Orthodox Church with its brilliant blue cupola, more houses, a shopping mall, gas stations, the post office.

Suddenly, Izzy stops and leans against a telephone pole, his forehead popping sweat. "Grandpa?" Rachel moves nearer. If he falls, can she catch him? She has an awful vision of Izzy crashing to the ground through her hands. "Grandpa," she says again. "Are you okay?"

He doesn't answer her, doesn't look at her. He's standing there, breathing in a way that makes Rachel understand breath as a thing in itself, as something which some people have for free and some people have to work for.

After a few minutes, which seem very long to Rachel, he nods, not to her, but to himself, takes off his cap, and wipes his forehead with a handkerchief. He nods and wipes his forehead. His lips are moving. "Okay," he says. She has to lean close to hear.

"Okay?" she says.

He folds his handkerchief carefully and tucks it in his pocket. "Okay."

"Should we start back?"

"Not yet."

They walk again. Rachel keeps looking at her grandfather. A couple of times she says, "Are you okay?"

"Stop asking me that."

She stops asking. She's obedient and she hates being obedient. She hates *this*. If he were healthy, she wouldn't choose to walk with him—she *wouldn't* walk with him. Why punish herself? But he's sick. And she's stuck. Every moment she's afraid he's going to fall. Once, he stumbles over a crack in the sidewalk and her hand flies out to steady him. He brushes her off.

When they enter the lobby of his building, the woman with purple hair is sitting on the wooden bench, knitting with long green needles. "Hello, Mr. Shapiro. I see you got a pretty friend visiting today."

Izzy nods. "This is my watchdog," he says, and he pushes the buzzer for the elevator.

NINETEEN

"So you'll come with us?" Helena says on Thursday as she and Rachel hurry to their chemistry class.

"Ummm . . ." Rachel begins.

"No umms!" Helena says firmly. "It's a half day—"

"It is?"

"Half day," Helena repeats. "It was on the PA yesterday. In-house meeting for all the lucky teachers. We're dismissed at one o'clock—and Mikey's dying to show off the car."

"Not to me."

"To anybody, Rache."

"I guess I qualify, then."

Mikey's new car is a green VW bug. When Rachel and Helena leave school, it's parked at the curb and Mikey is draped over the wheel. He beeps out a little welcome on the horn.

"And look who's in the backseat," Helena says.

It's Lewis, his knees jackknifed almost to his chin. "Hi, Mikey's cousin," Helena says to him. She and Mikey kiss.

Rachel slides into the backseat. "Hi," she says to Lewis. He raises his right eyebrow and his left hand in greeting.

Mikey turns around and gives Rachel his pilot-of-the-future smile. "Do you like this car, Rachel?"

"I do. Helena says your father just handed it over to you."

"He's letting me have it on certain conditions. You can guess what they are."

"Keeping up the grades," Helena says. She ticks them off on her fingers. "No accidents, no beer in the car, no booze in the car or anywhere else."

"You forgot paying for the gas and half the insurance," Mikey says. "Well, here we go, guys." He guns the engine and pulls away from the curb.

They drive around the city for a while with Mikey demonstrating the way the bug can whip in and out of traffic. Then Helena says, "Mikey, let's go somewhere. I don't want to just drive around like this. It's boring. You quiet ones in the backseat—you agree?"

"We'll go to Indian Falls Park." Mikey makes a U-turn.

"I don't think that was a very good place to make a U-turn," Helena says.

"Hey, you're starting to sound like Rachel."

"Oh, thank you. I take that as a compliment." Helena turns around. "You two are quiet as mice back there. Are you having a fight?"

Lewis and Rachel glance at each other. "Fight?" Lewis says. Somehow it comes out sounding like *Yes*.

"Oh, you guys," Helena says. "You are the worst—you both like to argue, don't you? Well, I don't want you fighting. You have to make up. Come on, which one of you is going to start?"

"Are you sorry?" Rachel asks Lewis.

"Why should I be sorry?"

"You know."

"Oh, that."

"Yes, *that.*"

110

"Well, if it's just *that*—"

"Did you think it was more than *that?*"

"Yes, I thought it was more than *that*. Did you think it was only *that?*"

Helena stares suspiciously from one to the other. "You two are putting me on, aren't you?"

"Us?" Lewis says.

"Helena . . ." Rachel says reproachfully.

"Oh, you—!" Helena leans over the seat and tries to box Rachel around the ears.

"Help. Help. Helena's on a rampage."

Lewis pretends to cower in a corner. "What an aggressive wench. We'll have no more of your violence here."

"What's the matter with him?" Mikey says.

Helena settles down next to Mikey again. "*Him* and my friend, there, are a pair of bad actors."

In the park they walk around for a while, then Mikey says he wants to see the fire tower and Rachel says she wants to see the falls. So Mikey and Helena go off in one direction and Lewis and Rachel in the other.

They go down the long, winding stairs cut into the cliff. Around a turn, the falls come into view. A long, narrow tumble of white foam over limestone ledges. They hang over the fence, watching the water. Lewis clasps Rachel's shoulder and says something. She can barely hear him over the noise of the falls. She turns toward him. "What?"

"Can I—" he yells. "Can we—" And he leans toward her fast, their lips bump, their teeth crash. For a moment, Rachel's not quite sure, then she is—it's a kiss. Lewis pulls back a little, she leans in a little, their arms go around each other.

That little voice in Rachel's head that has something to say about everything is ticking away.

Mmmm ... this is turning into a good kiss. ... How do you know that? Your vast experience? His lips are soft. He smells good. She puts her hand on his hair. The little voice comes on for a moment. *Check out his eyes ... open or closed? Good, they're closed ... better close yours.* She commands the voice to shut up and goes back to kissing.

Walking back up the path, she and Lewis hold hands and look at each other a lot and smile. "How do you feel about me?" Lewis says.

"Excellent. How do you feel about me?"

"Good."

"Just good?"

"Very good. Terrific. Terrifically excellent." Lewis drops into his Dr. Roof voice. "Vell, now ve have good, excellent feeling for each ozzer. Yessss, let me speak for myself. I have many feelings for you. Many varm, friendly feelings. Yesss, I am feeling this feeling and I am feeling that feeling, friendly feeling and varm feeling and saxual feeling."

"Ahh," Rachel says, and they kiss again. This is the way they continue the walk—talking, stopping, kissing, walking, stopping again, kissing again.

Then Rachel, in a little glow, thinking about how very nice kissing is—look what she's missed all these years!—asks, "Lewis, have you kissed a lot of girls?"

"Me? Uh, vell. Vhy do you ask?"

"I'm just curious," she says, but really it's more than that. To tell the truth, she's ready to be jealous. "So? Have you?"

"What iss your dafinition of *a lot?*"

"My dafinition is just like your dafinition." She frowns. The way he's avoiding answering tells her that he has kissed a lot of girls. She doesn't like that! "How many?" she says.

"How many vhat?"

"How many girls have you kissed?" Does she really want to know? Yes! Maybe the truth won't be as bad as what she's imagining, which is Lewis standing at the head of a long line of girls, all of them eagerly awaiting their turn to be kissed by him.

"Hey," Lewis says in his own voice. "What do you think?"

"How do I know? Probably dozens." As soon as she says it, another dismal idea strikes her. Has he been comparing her to the other girls he's kissed?

"Not exactly dozens," Lewis says.

"Oh. Well, what is the figure? One dozen?"

He shakes his head.

"More or less?"

"Uh. Less."

"Ten?"

Another shake of the head.

"Eight?"

"Does it matter?" Lewis tries to kiss her.

"Wait." She puts her hands against his chest, holds him off. "Lewis I don't want to be one of many, thank you very much." Her cheeks are flushed. She's trying to be dignified and sound reasonable, but she knows she's got That Look on her face.

"Rachel!" Lewis makes a grab for her hand and holds it. "Who said anything about many?"

"I think eight definitely qualifies as many!"

"You're the one who said that, Rachel, not me. Who do you think you're talking to? Emilio Estevez? Tom Cruise?" He pulls at his hair. "Let's not get crazy here. This is me, Lewis. You want to know the dead truth? I'm going to tell you. I've kissed two other girls in my entire lifetime."

"Oh," Rachel says. "Two?"

"Two. Isn't that pathetic? I wasn't going to tell

you that. I don't go around boasting about it, you know."

He looks unhappy. She can't stand it. He's unhappy because of her. She made him unhappy, asking him her dumb, jealous questions. She moves closer to him, puts her hands around his face and kisses him.

When they return to the car, Helena and Mikey are waiting for them. "Where have you two been?"

"Talking," says Rachel.

"Howling at the moon," says Lewis.

TWENTY

"Where were you?" her grandfather says to Rachel over the phone. "I waited for you."

"What?"

"Do you think I have nothing else to do?"

"What?" she repeats stupidly.

"Why didn't you call me if you weren't coming?"

"You were expecting me today? Grandpa, I-I was working. I work on Thursdays."

"I stayed in all day, waiting for you." His voice is thin-edged, cutting.

"I-I'm sorry," she stammers.

"I'll see you tomorrow," he says, and hangs up.

Rachel stands in the kitchen with the phone in her hand. Her heart suddenly pounds with anger and panic. The tyrant, the awful old tyrant. All right! She'll walk with him tomorrow. And then what? Is he going to expect her on Saturday, too? Not Sunday, because he has them *all* under his thumb on Sunday. But what happens on Monday? And Tuesday? And every other day after that? Is she supposed to go and walk with him every day?

What was it he said to her? "Do you think I have nothing else to do but wait for you?" And what about her? What about her life? Yes, yes, a voice jeers in her head, that's the way, you selfish, cold heart, compare yourself to an old, dying man. And then, coolly, the voice reminds her that while she did, indeed, go to work, before that she had plenty of time to drive around with her friends, have fun, and kiss Lewis in the park.

She goes to Izzy's house the next afternoon, straight from school. They walk at his snail's pace. He seems to be all right. His breathing is actually better than the first day she walked with him. He doesn't even have to stop to wipe his forehead. Breath for walking but no breath for talking. What does she expect, anyway? She's just his watchdog. Arf! Arf!

When she leaves him, she feels as if she's escaped from prison, and she says to herself, That's it. No more. Ma will just have to get somebody else to baby-sit him.

At supper, her father asks her about the afternoon. "Where did you go with Grandpa, Mouse?"

She sighs over the awful nickname and says, "Oh, we just walked around, Daddy. I followed Grandpa. I think he has these routes he's got worked out. He seems to know exactly where he wants to go."

"Well, Izzy would," her father says with a smile.

"Right," Rachel says, and sits up straighter to tell her parents that today was the last time she'll watchdog her grandfather. "Ma? I don't want to, uh—" She hesitates. Should she just say it like that, or soften it a little?

"Rachey—" Her mother leans toward her. "It's so wonderful that you're doing this. All day I thought about how you'd be there when he went out walking. You don't know what a relief it is to me to know you're with him." Her mother's eyes are wet and glowing. "Thank you, sweetheart."

After that, what can Rachel say?

In school the next day, Lewis catches her in the

116

hall. "Doing anything later? We could go some-where, do something." He looks hopeful.

They stand by the foot of the stairs and Rachel tells him about Izzy. "Oh," Lewis says. "Sure." The bell rings and reluctantly he lets go of her hand.

When Rachel approaches Building C later, she sees Izzy waiting for her in the lobby. He's standing straight, hands clasped behind his back, turtle eyes fixed on her as she pushes open the glass door. She's dead on time, but his greeting is, "So, you finally got here."

Outside, a bunch of little girls are practicing cheers in the parking lot. "We are the BEE-EE-ESS-TEE, best! Forget about the ARE-EE-ESS-TEE, rest!" They get down on their knees, throw out their arms, their voices ragged.

Past the little girls Rachel and Izzy go, up the street, slow, slow, slow, like two ancient lizards. The muscles in Rachel's legs start twitching almost at once from moving so slowly. Maybe she's practicing to be old. This is the way she'll walk when her legs are gone, when she can't get down on her knees like those little girls anymore, when she can't pedal a bike, when she's bowlegged and bent. She thinks it, but she doesn't believe it, can't imagine being old. A shudder passes over her. She remembers an old woman she saw at the bus stop, bent so far over that her back was parallel to the ground.

Izzy turns a corner, crosses a street. Rachel is aware they're avoiding the hills but otherwise hardly knows where they're going. She follows Izzy. The breath softly whistles or wheezes in and out of his chest.

For a while she works on a story in her head. Then she thinks about Lewis. She goes back to the story. Maybe she'll weave in this really nice boy.

Tall. Thin. Narrow and skinny. What would be his role in the story? Maybe the parents wouldn't like him. Or maybe they'd like him so much, it would really irritate the girl. Her mind drifts off. It's hard to think this way. And if nobody says anything, she will soon die of BEE-OH-ARE-EE-DEE-OH-EMM!

"We didn't go down this street yesterday, Grandpa."

"Mmm-huh."

"Is this a new route for you?"

"New route?"

"New way of walking."

"No."

Now they are passing Schuyler Hill, and Rachel thinks of Alice Farnum with the silver sparkles on her cheek. "Grandpa?"

"Mmm-huh."

"Did you ever speak to Alice Farnum again?"

"Mmm-huh."

"You did?"

"Mmm-huh."

"You called her?"

"No."

"She called you?"

"Mmm-huh."

"So how was that?"

"How should it be?"

"I liked her."

To this, she doesn't even get an *Mmm-huh.*

When they return, the purple-haired woman is at her usual post in the lobby. "How are we today, Mr. Shapiro? Hello, darling. Did you and Grandpa have a nice walk?"

"Good day, Mrs. Patton." Izzy pushes the button

for the elevator. And, "Good-bye," he says to Rachel.

"I'll go up with you."

"No, you won't." The elevator creaks open. He steps in. The door closes and he's gone. Maybe he's a dying man, but he's still Izzy.

TWENTY-ONE

All through the next week, Rachel walks with her grandfather. Every day it's the same thing. She goes to the Loren Towers directly from school. He's waiting for her in the lobby. She says hello. He grunts. They go out and walk for about an hour. They may exchange a few awkward remarks about the weather or they may say nothing at all. At the end of the hour, they're back at the Loren Towers. And Izzy says, with an offhand shrug, "I suppose you're coming tomorrow?" As if her walking with him is something she wants, and has nothing to do with him.

Another week passes, filled with the same slow, tedious walks, the same random, pointless remarks about the weather and the traffic. Every day it's Rachel's leg muscles twitching, it's Izzy's breath wheezing and whistling. And every evening it's Shirley sitting down with Rachel and asking, "How was he? Is he breathing the same? Did you notice any change?"

Shirley asks these questions as if Rachel is the expert, and Rachel can't help liking that part of her job. That's the way she's beginning to think of it—as her second, but unpaid, job. Still, every day, at some point, she's fed up and she stumps along next to Izzy, frowning and thinking, *I've had it. I didn't see*

Lewis today because of this. *Yesterday I was supposed to go to Helena's and I couldn't. No, this is it. Today is absolutely the last time I'm doing this.*

And then they return to Izzy's house, he rings for the elevator, and he says to her, "I suppose you're coming tomorrow?" And no matter how hard her thoughts have been, the fact that he's asking—that it's her grandfather, that it's *Izzy* asking something of her—works on her every time, like hot water over ice.

"So, Grandpa," Rachel says, "I've got a question for you. Do you like having me walk with you?"

"I don't mind."

That might be taken as a compliment, coming from Izzy, but Rachel isn't on a fishing expedition. She's got something else on her mind. She wants to know why, for going on two weeks, he's not only accepted her presence on his walks but also expects it. It's so un-Izzyish. The only days she's excused are Thursdays when she works and Sundays when the whole family goes to his place.

"You used to walk alone."

"Mmm-huh."

Oh, those *Mmm-huh*s of his! She'd like to outlaw them. She'd like to stuff them in a bag and ship them to Siberia. She'd like to tell him, Grandpa, you sound like an aardvark when you say mmm-huh, mmm-huh, mmm-huh!

"I know you're not afraid of falling again," she says.

He gives her a look that should warn her.

She goes on, "Because Ma says you said—"

"Ma says you said," he mimics.

Oh. Oh. Oh. *Oh!* How is it that in an instant, Izzy can make her forget everything—her manners, his age, that he's a dying man? "Ma says you said," she persists, "that you *know* you're not going to fall again."

He takes off his cap, wipes his forehead with a handkerchief. "Only a fool takes anything for granted. I've been called a lot of things in my life . . . but never a fool."

Then he doesn't say anything else for the rest of the walk, but Rachel has had her question answered. If not afraid of falling, Izzy at least considers it a real possibility. Which leads to another question. Does that mean he knows something they think he doesn't know—just how sick he is?

Walking with her grandfather gets no easier. It's—to put it plainly—boring. They walk so slowly, they see nothing of interest, they talk about nothing of interest. Rachel doesn't want to hear about the weather. She's *in* the weather, that's good enough for her. She doesn't want to hear about the dirty streets and traffic jams. Her brain is getting jammed.

"Sometimes," she tells Helena, "I feel as if I'm sleepwalking."

"You know, you could use the time."

"*Use* the time? God, Helena! I can't believe you said that. What am I supposed to do, crossword puzzles? We're walking, we're outdoors, we're crawling along like two old lizards—"

"You're sputtering," Helena says. They're eating lunch together and she passes Rachel a napkin. "Wipe," she orders, pointing to Rachel's mouth. "What I meant was, why not make a sort of project of it. Find out things about your grandfather. Sort of an oral-history thing."

"You're such a blooming Girl Scout," Rachel

says, tearing the napkin into shreds. "If I didn't like you, I really wouldn't like you."

"Thank you, my love."

"Grandpa, do you think about Grandma Eva a lot?"

"Eh?"

"I don't know much about her."

"She's dead."

"I do know that," she says.

"Leave the dead in peace."

"Come on, Grandpa," Rachel cries, "give a little, will you?" She's desperate. Why tiptoe around Izzy? You don't get any points from him that way. You don't get anything from him that way. "Tell me something! *Anything*. How long were you married?"

"A long time." He pulls up the collar of his jacket. It's cool today and he's wearing a heavy wool jacket. "Married when we were seventeen," he says.

"Young," Rachel says. She waits for more. Nothing is forthcoming. They turn a corner. She is getting to know these streets better than the ones in her own neighborhood. "You know what?" she says. "I bet you have a lot of things you can tell me." An unashamed appeal to his vanity.

"What things?"

"Oh," she says, "all about your life, Grandpa. Tell me where you lived when you were growing up."

"Right here. Oak Street."

"I didn't know that." She shouldn't have said it. Now he will say, "Now you know."

"Now you know," he says.

"What was Ma like when she was a little girl? How about Uncle Leonard—"

Oops. That's it. She's just slipped on the banana peel. She shouldn't have mentioned Uncle Leonard. Izzy's lips thin. "What is this, Twenty Questions?"

They cross the street, walk down a little sloping hill past a playing field. A soccer game is in progress and the crowd is yelling in English and Italian. "You want to stop and watch the game?" she says.

He doesn't. They proceed on. He says nothing else. So much for the oral-history project.

Thursday after school and before she goes to work, Lewis and Rachel stop in at Poppie's, a diner on Canal Street. "Poppie's a friend of Louise's," Lewis says.

"Who's Louise?"

"My older sister."

"That's the first time you've mentioned her."

"There are a lot of things I don't know about you, either."

"Well, I know one thing about you," she says in a happy voice, thinking about how he kisses.

"Oh." He must be thinking about the same thing, because he smiles and blushes. "Yeah, Louise is married, she lives in Rochester. She teaches and she's got two babies."

"So you're an uncle. Did you know I'm an aunt?"

"My God, we're two old farts."

They walk up the steps and into the diner. A young woman with short hair is behind the counter, chopping onions. "Hey, Lewis." She's wearing a blouse, a dark cardigan, and jeans.

"Poppie." Lewis leans on the counter. "This is my friend Rachel."

"Hi, Rachel."

"Hello." She looks around. "I like this place."

"Thanks, I do, too," Poppie says. Besides the

usual menus on the wall above the counter, there are also kids' drawings and taped-up cartoons. The whole place is very small, half a dozen booths, maybe ten stools at the counter.

"You guys going to sit down and eat, or what?"

"Eat," Lewis says, "definitely eat."

In the booth, they sit next to each other, their shoulders touching, eating and talking. The talk gets around to Izzy.

"I read that people who are dying sometimes know it," Lewis says. "Even if nobody's told them in so many words. The idea is that somehow their body is telling them. Giving them signals."

"I wonder if my grandfather knows."

"He probably knows more than you think. Maybe he even knows more than he knows he knows."

"I think you're right," she says.

"Rachel? Is this Rachel? It's Alice Farnum. Am I calling too late?"

"No, that's fine, I just got home from work. I was just talking about you to my grandfather the other day."

"I think about you both a lot. How's your grandfather getting on? I talked to him once right after that day, but I didn't want to ask him too much. I didn't want to upset him, and I wasn't sure . . . well, let me tell you the reason I'm calling you. Last night, I had a dream I just had to tell you about."

"Yes?" Rachel says, as if people always call her up and tell them their dreams.

"I was dancing, there was a wooden rail around a grassy area, and I was dancing on the grass. Your grandfather was there, sitting on the railing. At first, I was so happy, then a sadness came over me. I looked over, your grandfather was gone, but you

125

were there. I knew I should be happy to see you, I *was* happy to see you, but there was something very sad—I woke up feeling sad, and I thought, 'I must call Rachel.' I think the dream was trying to tell me something. Do you think so, Rachel?"

"Well . . . yes."

"What is it? What is it about your grandfather? You know why he fell down now, don't you?"

"Yes. It's—kind of serious."

"I was afraid of that. I'm so sorry."

TWENTY-TWO

JOURNAL •

Friday night. Today, when I got to Grandpa's, I knew right away that he was in a bad mood. He had these little eyes and his eyebrows were going off in every direction. We went out. He walked faster than usual. I thought he was pushing himself.

I said, "We're really stepping out today." He didn't say anything. I said, "It was cold last night." No answer. "Did they turn on the heat in your building yet?" Nothing.

At first, this mood of his really intimidated me. I wanted to get the walk over with, get away from him and let him have his rotten mood to himself. Then, gradually, I don't know why exactly, my thoughts or my feelings shifted around. I think I started feeling sorry—that he was coughing and wheezing, that he couldn't keep on walking fast. Something like that. And this idea came to me: Maybe he doesn't like being in a crummy mood any more than *I* do when it happens to me.

So I thought, Well, I'll try to get him out of it, and I started talking about Martin, my boss. At first, it was the same thing. I talked, Grandpa grunted. Forget it! I gave up. What was the use? So then we were both not talking. And then suddenly Grandpa says, "What's this so-called job?"

"So-called? It's not so-called. It's a job. I'm a bag girl."

"Bad girl?"

"Bag. *GGGG*. Bag girl."

"I'm not deaf, Rachel. What's a bag girl?"

"You know, when you go to the supermarket and somebody packs your groceries? That's me."

"You do that? What for?"

"What do you mean, what for?"

"What for? What for? *Why?*"

"*Why?* You mean, why do I do it? To earn money!"

"What do they pay you?"

"Minimum wage."

"Pfaaa!"

That was our big conversation. Then he clammed up again. I think to myself, What was that all about? And the only thing I'm glad of is that he wasn't the only snapping turtle in that exchange.

I'm walking along with him, giving him little sideways looks and thinking about this and that. About Lewis, about work, writing, et cetera. And I suppose without my even realizing it, Grandpa's there in my head, too, because suddenly I thought, Oh, *right!* And I understood exactly why he was in such a bad mood. I wanted to slap myself on the head for not figuring it out sooner. It's so simple, really. Thursday, I work. So Grandpa doesn't walk. Which makes him feel mad or bad, one or the other, or maybe both.

I said, "Grandpa, did you go out at all yesterday?" He gave me one of his grunts, an *mmmm* without the *huh*. It could have been yes or it could have been no. But I'm pretty sure it was no.

Saturday. Today, walking with Grandpa, we passed that enormous blue spruce on the corner. We pass it every day. I always look at it. Grandpa said, "I watched that tree grow."

I said, "I like that tree. How tall do you think it is?"

"Forty feet."

"How old is it?"

"Not as old as me."

Monday. I asked Grandpa if he and my grandmother did a lot of walking together. He said, "Who walked?" And he did that wave of his hand that means, Don't bother me! But then, without my even coaxing him, he went on talking. "Those days, I worked. Eva was busy with the house, the children. Who heard of walking for enjoyment?"

"How about for exercise?"

He looked at me, one of those sly, from-the-corner-of-his-eye looks, and he said, "Exercise is a modern invention."

I started laughing, and he looked really pleased with himself. "Mmm-huh," he said, "mmm-huh."

TWENTY-THREE

Izzy isn't in the lobby waiting for Rachel when she arrives. She runs up the stairs, wondering, starting to get frightened. She raises her hand to knock, then thinks maybe he's taking a nap. But immediately she thinks something else. Yes, he's sleeping, but he won't wake up, can't wake up, will never wake up—and her breath mimics his, crowding her chest.

A woman in slippers, carrying a soggy bag in her arms, passes and gives Rachel a close look. "You want something?" Rachel shakes her head. Does she look like a suspicious character? The woman drops her garbage into the incinerator and walks away, looking back over her shoulder several times.

Rachel listens at Izzy's door, hears nothing. She knocks, a light tap. She raps a little harder, then tries the doorknob. "Grandpa. Grandpa?"

Izzy opens the door. He's in slippers, wearing a faded plaid bathrobe over his shirt and pants. "Oh. It's you."

She walks into the apartment. A blanket is rucked up at the foot of the couch. He sits down heavily. "I didn't have such a good night." His eyes are small, the whites streaked with red. "I didn't sleep so much."

"Maybe you don't want to go out for a walk

today—" She breaks off. Izzy has fallen asleep, sitting up.

"Uhh?" His head jerks to one side. His eyes open. He stares around with a fearful look. "What is it?" he says hoarsely. His nose is sweating.

Rachel brings him a glass of water. "Do you want to rest a little more, Grandpa?" She sits down on the couch next to him.

He gulps the water, wipes his mouth. "No. No, I'm going out." He takes his wallet from a side table, opens it. "I'll do a little shopping." He counts out a few bills.

Later, at home, she remembers his hands. Thick, gray, shaking.

Two little girls in jeans, ribbons bouncing on the ends of their braids, come out of an apartment on Izzy's floor. "Hiiii," they chorus to Rachel.

"Hi," Rachel says.

"You live here?" the smaller girl says. She has one front tooth missing.

Rachel shakes her head.

"What's your name?"

"Rachel. What's yours?"

"Darlene. And this here is my sister Traci."

"Hi, Darlene. Hi, Traci."

"Don't mind Darlene," Traci says.

"You go to school?" Darlene says.

"Darlene asks too many questions," Traci says. She has fat, shining cheeks. "All she does all day is ask questions. She drives me crazy."

"You like to be late to school?" Darlene puts her hands in her back pockets. "I like to be late to school. I like detention. Who you seeing here?"

"Darlene, shut up."

"My grandfather."

"Who's he?"

"Dar-leeeeene!"

"Mr. Shapiro."

"Oh, the mean man."

"Dar-leeeeene! He is not."

"He is, too. What do you know, Traci? He has mean faces."

The elevator arrives. "Bye, Rachel," they both yell, getting in.

That day, the mean man and Rachel walk to the Jewish cemetery where her grandmother is buried. At different times through the years Rachel has come here with her mother. The gravestones date back over a hundred years. The cemetery, at the end of a narrow street crowded with small houses, is hidden by a fieldstone wall. A wrought-iron Star of David rises above the gate. Izzy bends over, looking at the wall. Rachel sees nothing but stones, moss, dried-up leaves. "What are you looking at?"

"I'm looking at good work. Look at this . . . wall. Straight, solid, like the day it was built." He breathes for a moment. "You see the way the stones fit?"

Rachel examines the wall. "They seem to fit okay."

"Not okay. Good. Very good."

Something about his tone catches her attention, some little note of pride or possession. "Grandpa, did you build this wall?"

He looks at her. "I fixed it. This is an old . . . wall. It was falling down and I fixed it." He bends over again. "You see this? This wall has almost no mud."

"It's not muddy at all," Rachel says.

"You don't know what I mean, huh?"

"You said it wasn't muddy and I said—"

"I said mud, not muddy. Mud. You don't know what mud is?" He's laughing at her.

"Of course I know what mud is "

"No, you don't. It's cement. It's what they put between the stones. Today, they spread it everywhere like peanut butter. Because today ..." He pauses. "... today, they have machines. Cement mixers. You pull a lever ... and you have cement, coming out like soft ice cream." He takes out his handkerchief, wipes his mouth. "The hard work is the stones. Mud is easy. Stones are hard. ... So they use too much mud. You understand?"

"Yes, I do now."

"When I started at this, the hard work was the mud. Harder than stones ... Everything had to be mixed ... by hand. Heavy work." The long speech is using his breath. "So you didn't ... waste mud." He leans against the wall, breathing. "You ... used less."

Rachel hoists herself up onto the wall. She runs her hands over the top of the stones the same way he did. "Did you always work on walls?"

"At first, I worked on nothing. I only mixed mud. I carried it to the bricklayers. I was an apprentice. I was fifteen ... doing a man's work. The worst jobs, that's what the apprentices ... get. Everybody yells and you run. You better be strong." He stops, his hand wanders over his chest, as though he's wondering what's going on in there. "Five years before they let me put a hand on stone. You know Clearbrook ... Creek?"

"Clearbrook Road? I go to school that way."

"I said Clearbrook Creek. How do you think the road got its name? The brook runs under it. Some places, it runs next to it ... you ever notice that?"

"I guess so."

"Don't guess so. Yes or no?"

"Yes!"

"You ever see the bridges . . . where the road crosses the creek? I built every one of those bridges."

"I didn't know that."

"Now you . . . do." He almost doesn't get the last word out. He starts coughing and then wheezing, his face suffuses, his chest rattles alarmingly. Rachel hops off the wall. How easily she hops around, how easily she clears her throat and breathes, how smoothly, how effortlessly she does it all.

She stands near him, would like to hold his arm, at least, but knows better. All she is allowed is to stand by and wait for the coughing, the wheezing, the rattling to subside.

He spits, wipes his mouth, breathes. "Okay," he says, "okay. Let's go in."

In the cemetery, they walk slowly up the hill between the rows of stones. Drifts of leathery leaves cover the paths. He stops at her grandmother's grave, a small flat stone: EVA DEVONSKI SHAPIRO, DEVOTED WIFE, BELOVED MOTHER. He kneels down, brushes at the stone. A wind springs up, whips Rachel's hair around her face.

In the west, the sky is turning a clear, cold blue. Rachel stands very still, watching Izzy. How odd to see him this way, on his knees. He keeps brushing the stone, brushing away twigs and bits of leaves. "You told me not to come here, so I don't," he says. Then he says something else, low; Rachel can't make it out. A smile crosses his lips, he nods his head.

Is he talking to her grandmother? A shiver takes Rachel by the neck, shakes her like a dog shaking a bone. The dead—and their spirits?—are all around.

134

She bends over Izzy, touches his arm urgently. He looks up at her. His eyes are gray as water-washed pebbles, bleached and distant. "Should we go, Grandpa? It's getting dark."

He unwinds himself with a groan. She takes his arm to help him up, and he allows it; his arm trembles under hers. They go back down through the rows of graves. It's dusk, the trees are flat, black lacy patterns against a greenish sky. On the street, houses are lit up, cars approach, their headlights glowing dimly. Rachel and Izzy move along without speaking.

"What's the use?" Izzy says at last, and his face takes on its familiar, remote look. All the same, when Rachel leaves him, for the first time she kisses him good-bye.

"Don't come in with me," Izzy instructs Rachel. They're in front of the little market a couple blocks from his house.

"Grandpa, I'll wheel the cart for you."

"I'll wheel my own cart. Stay out here."

"I want to buy something for myself. I want an apple."

"I'll buy it for you."

"I want to choose my own apple."

"What makes you so stubborn?"

"Look who's talking."

Inside, he pushes the cart. "Get me a can of sardines. . . . Get me a box of cornflakes. Get me raisins." Now that she's there, he orders her around as if shopping is unmanly. "Milk. And don't get me that two-percent stuff, it tastes like chalk."

At the checkout counter, he peels a ten-dollar bill off a small roll.

"Have a good one," the cashier says, putting the raisins in the bag. Rachel goes for the bag, but Izzy brushes her aside, picks it up.

She follows him outside. "Would you just let me carry that, please?"

"No."

"Why?"

Already he's breathing too hard. "I can carry my own . . . groceries."

"I know you can," she argues. "I didn't say you couldn't. But you could just let me do it today."

"Be quiet. Stop bothering me." He carries the bag all the way back. In the lobby, he sits down on the bench but doesn't give up the bag. Sits there and breathes.

When he gets on the elevator, he holds up his hand for her to stay back. The elevator door closes. She watches the dial moving sluggishly from one to two. Suddenly, she is so angry that her head feels as if it's on fire. Izzy is like that elevator door: opening for a moment, then closing in her face. She can't just go away, leave; she has to tell him something. She runs up the stairs, making a speech in her head.

Would it be too much to ask that you at least say good-bye to me? It's rude not to, but it's more than that. I have this weird, unfinished feeling when you leave me like that. And tell me this, why didn't you let me help you carry the groceries? And what's wrong with my going up in the elevator with you?

She arrives on the third floor just as Izzy is getting out of the elevator. He doesn't see her coming from the stairs. He's talking—she thinks to someone in one of the apartments, but there's no one around, no one else in the hall. He's talking to himself.

"Yeah," he says. "Yeah, that's good, Izzy. . . . Good . . . good. . . . You did it." He laughs briefly. "Passed the test."

From the stairs, she watches him unlock his door, go inside. Then she goes back down the stairs.

TWENTY-FOUR

It's drizzling when Rachel leaves school. By the time she gets to Izzy's house, the rain is coming down hard. "Mmm, so it's you," her grandfather says when she walks in.

"Expecting anybody else?" She shakes out her jacket. "I guess we can't go out today."

"Then why did you come?"

Rachel stops in the act of taking off her damp sneakers. Why *did* she come? Multiple-choice test. One: to see Izzy. Two: to annoy Izzy. Three: to walk with Izzy. Four: to check up on Izzy. Answer: All of the above. Besides, by now she's not just a watchdog, she's a trained watchdog, and when the last bell rings in school, she automatically heads in this direction.

"Maybe the rain will stop in a while, Grandpa."

"Mmm-huh."

The apartment is overheated. Rachel rolls up the sleeves of her sweater and stands at the window. The sky is full of dark clouds. A slash of lightning brightens the sky, thunder rattles the window.

"Grandpa, since we can't go out, we should do something exciting. How about a game of Scrabble?"

"You know how to play?"

"Sure. It's easy."

He gets out the game. Rachel fashions flashy words, makes quick moves. Izzy takes his time, plays the game like chess, lots of deliberation. He wins by a considerable score. "Uh-ha, uh-ha," he says. "And I never went past the eighth grade."

His smile annoys her. "I'll beat you next time." She's serious. She doesn't like losing.

"You want another game right now?"

"You bet!"

She plays harder this time, mulls over her options, goes for points instead of the showy stuff. He wins again with a seven-letter word that gives him fifty extra points and takes him over the top. "A lot of little tricks of the game you don't know," he says. "I'll show you."

"Never mind, I'll win the next time."

"You can try," he says.

The phone rings. Izzy takes it. "Hello! Yes. . . . Yes . . . okay." He hangs up, his eyes are sly. "The inspector says, don't go home until the storm stops."

"The inspector?"

"Your mother, the Inspector General," he says, enjoying his joke.

"Ma worries about storms, Grandpa."

"Sure, she does. She gets that from her mother. You know what my Eva did when there was a storm? Can you guess?" He's looking at her expectantly. She shakes her head. "She hid in the closet. The only thing she was afraid of. Are you?"

"Afraid of storms? No. I like them."

"You're like me," he says.

"Are you afraid of anything?"

He shrugs. "I just do what I do."

"Are you afraid of dying?" Her stomach dives. She didn't know she was going to say that. Why did she say it? *Are you afraid of dying?* There's no taking back the words—they're out, they won't go away, they lie there, between her and Izzy, like blocks of wood she's thrown down with a careless thump.

His leg jerks in a muscle spasm. "Everybody dies." He bends over, massaging his knee.

Does he know? She can't see his face.

"Why be afraid of that?" His voice is dry. "You're born, you live, you die."

Outside, it's completely dark. Torrents of rain pour down the windows. The clock in the kitchen ticks erratically. It's losing time, needs to be fixed.

The sky clears overnight, and the next day is a perfect fall day—warm with blue skies and the air smelling of smoke and leaves. Rachel expects Izzy to be waiting impatiently in the lobby. He's not there.

At his door, she knocks and hears nothing. She knocks again, listens, waits. For days on end, she forgets, really, the underlying reason she's at his house so much, forgets that he's a dying man, forgets that his time is limited and passing. Now she remembers.

She raps harder, rattles the doorknob, and looks around. Where will she go for help? Which door will she knock on first? Then she hears the floor creaking and his slow footfall and the tumbling of the three locks. Izzy looks out at her. His hair is mussed, he's in a sleeveless undershirt. She sees the creases in his face, his puffy eyes. "You're here? What time is it?"

She feels stupid with relief. "I'm here." She makes an awkward grab for his hand and kisses it.

TWENTY-FIVE

JOURNAL •

Wednesday. Today, Grandpa tried to walk up Schuyler Hill. We stopped at the foot of the hill. He looked up at it like it was Mt. Everest. "Well, let's give this a try." We started up. It was step, step, step. He got his hands down on his knees, pushing forward, stooped over and breathing like an old engine.

Not even halfway up, he stopped to rest. Then he couldn't keep going. He didn't say anything, just turned and started back down. But I know he felt awful. And so did I, for him.

Friday. Grandpa got tired pretty fast today. We were only out about twenty minutes and we had to sit down so he could rest. We sat on a bench at a bus stop. I had some jelly beans in my pocket. I held out my hand. "Want some?" He picked out a few of the black ones. "I like licorice, too," I said.

"You're not like your grandmother. She only liked sweet things. Sugary things. Box of candy was her favorite birthday present."

"What was she like?"

"I just told you."

"There was more to her than her sweet tooth, Grandpa."

"She was beautiful."

"You mean her looks?"

"What else are you talking about? She was beautiful. A beautiful little woman."

"Well, what kind of person was she?"

"Hardworking."

"Was she like my mother?"

"What way?"

"I think Ma is kind of high-strung. She's sensitive and nervous. She gets upset easily."

"Eva was not a nervous person. No. She was strong. She was strong." He repeated this a few times.

"Do you mean strong like this?" I lifted my arm, made a muscle.

"No, no, she was a little woman. A beautiful little woman. We went through a lot and she was always strong. She never broke down."

"How long were you married?"

"Fifty years. A week before she died, we had our fiftieth anniversary."

I shut up. I thought it made him sad. I thought about Grandma, and I felt sad that she had died before I was even born.

Saturday. This morning, Ma said at breakfast, "I had such a strong dream about my father. He was running, Mouse. Running so fast, I couldn't catch up with him." She was smiling and happy, telling the dream. Then she said the same thing she's said before. "I think he's going to fool all those doctors. He's going to live to be a hundred." And I believed her!

I began thinking about all the things Grandpa does that don't sound like somebody dying. Like eating pickles and playing killer Scrabble and washing out his socks every night—I thought of a hundred little things he does. Is that dying? It seems to me it's more like living.

Sunday. I slept over at Helena's last night. I talked to her for a long time about Grandpa and the things he told me about Grandma. Helena said, "Married fifty years—I think that's pretty impressive."

I agreed with her, then I realized that Ma and Daddy have been married almost as long, forty-five years. As soon as I thought it, I changed the subject. I didn't want to say that. I didn't want to draw attention to how old they are. We were talking about a movie we want to see. But all the time I was bothered because I hadn't said that about Ma and Daddy. I was annoyed with myself. It made me feel as if I were ashamed of them. So I said, "Did you know my parents have been married forty-five years?"

"Really?"

"Yeah." I was all tensed up for some remark. She could have said her mother wasn't even forty-five years old. All she said was, "I wonder if I'll ever get married."

I was surprised. Helena? "Of course you will."

"Why of course? Maybe I don't want to get married. I've heard you say you might not get married."

"I know, but that's me."

"I think I might. But I want to be an actress. If you got married, Rachel, what kind of a guy would you want?"

"One with a sense of humor. Also intelligent." I thought of Lewis. I really like him. Maybe I love him. But I can't see being married to him. I imagined us wearing pajamas and brushing our teeth together in the morning.

"What's funny?" Helena said.

I couldn't tell her. I rolled over and buried my face in the pillow.

Helena jumped on the bed and shook me. "What are you giggling about? What's the joke? Tell, Rachel! Or else!"

Then I said, sort of gasped out, "I was thinking—about—Lewis."

"Marrying Lewis?" she shrieked.

"And you—marrying—Mikey."

She shrieked again. "Fifty years with Mikey?"

"Fifty years—with Lewis—"

We couldn't stop laughing.

I said, "Could I last fifty years with somebody?"

Helena said, "Correction. Could somebody last fifty years with *you?*"

Tuesday. I don't know exactly when this started, but I always kiss Grandpa now when I see him, and then I kiss him again when I leave. Today, when I got to the house, he was in the lobby, talking to Mrs. Patton. "Hello, Grandpa."

"A-ha! Here's the kisser." And he held up his cheek for my kiss.

TWENTY-SIX

"Rachel!" A big woman unfolds herself from a car. It's Alice Farnum, wearing blue pants, a turquoise jacket, a blue turban. She runs up, hugs Rachel, enfolds her in big, warm arms. Then turns to Izzy. "Let me look at you, Mr. Shapiro." She gives him a hug, a long, radiant look.

Izzy is happy to see Alice. No, Rachel thinks, not happy, *delighted.* He doesn't mind at all that she's arrived just as they are starting out for their walk. He doesn't mind at all missing the walk. Not today. He takes Alice's arm. Like a gentleman, he walks her into the building, holds the elevator door open for her. In his apartment, he brings her a glass of cranberry juice, a little cup of peanuts, a napkin. He can't take his eyes off her.

"So this is where you live!" she says. "You've got a green thumb, Mr. Shapiro."

"What's with the Mr. Shapiro? Izzy, please." He holds out his hands. "Green thumbs? Not me. Gray thumbs. These thumbs were in cement dust most of my life. The plants were my wife's. They're all from her."

The windowsill is crowded with small and medium-sized plants, while the corner beyond the table holds all the big ones. Rachel has never paid much attention to them before, and now she's hearing that they're older than she is.

"I water once a week," Izzy says. "And I clean the leaves and I feed them once a month. Eva trained me. When she was dying, she said two things. She didn't want me visiting her grave and crying over her. She said, 'Once a year is enough. You can come and remember me, remember the nice things, that's okay.' And then she said, 'Don't let my plants die.'"

How easily Izzy is talking to Alice! And he's telling her things he's never told Rachel. He doesn't even know Rachel's there anymore. She goes into the kitchen and washes her grandfather's lunch dishes. Cinderella on the job. She splashes water into the sink, hangs up the pots with little thumps and clatters.

Izzy and Alice talk about the places they've lived, the jobs they've had. "I always thought I'd be a dancer with a famous company," Alice says in her clear, carrying voice. "But maybe I didn't have the dedication. Or maybe I wasn't good enough. So now I teach classes and rescue men who fall down on the sidewalk in front of my house."

Izzy laughs. Rachel yanks the garbage pail out of the can and carries it out to the incinerator.

"I've done plenty of other things besides stone-masonry," Izzy is saying, when Rachel returns. "If work was slow and we needed money, I would do whatever I had to. . . ." Rachel sweeps the kitchen floor. "I've worked on the railroad . . . on construction gangs with a pick and shovel. I've cleaned toilets on train platforms."

She wipes the stove and the top of the refrigerator. Now Alice is saying she's been a waitress, a cashier, a manager of a movie theater. "I have your philosophy, Izzy. I'll do whatever I need to, to support my dancing. Once I worked in a funeral parlor. I never went near the bodies, I didn't have the license, but still, every night while I worked there, I dreamed about dead people. I had to leave that job."

Rachel takes the dust mop from the closet and goes into Izzy's little bedroom. She lies down on the floor and pushes the dust mop around under the bed. All that talking! Yak! Yak! Yak! Izzy will be hoarse and wheezy by the time Alice leaves. She thrusts the dust mop into the corners.

When Alice leaves, Izzy gives her one of his plants, a big glossy jade that's almost like a little tree. She has to put both arms around it. "Are you sure? It's so beautiful."

"Take it. Take it. I don't need it."

"You're sweet." Alice kisses him. And Izzy, that traitor, kisses her back.

TWENTY-SEVEN

"Ma and Daddy are both working late tonight," Rachel says.

"Mmm-huh."

"Not that I couldn't make my own supper."

"Mmm-huh." Izzy cracks two eggs into a bowl. Rachel hands him another egg. "More food, please! I'm hungry at night, Grandpa."

"Get out the green pepper and an onion."

Yes, her parents are working late, but the real reason she's eating supper with Izzy is to report back to her mother what and how much he eats. Her mother is worried. "I know he's lost weight. I just look at his face and I know it."

Rachel cuts tomatoes, lettuce, peels a carrot. She finds a box of spaghetti in the cupboard, puts water on to boil, looks around to see what else she can have. "You want bread, Grandpa?"

"Not me."

"I do."

"So, have."

They carry the food to the table, sit down. Rachel's hungry and eats the eggs with enjoyment. "You know, Grandpa," she says, "you gave Alice cranberry juice when she was here."

"I did," he agrees.

"You served it to her. That was really nice."

"She was a guest. You always give guests something. . . . Don't you know that?"

"Yes, but . . ." She wants to say something that's been on her mind. "You've never done anything like that for Ma."

"What are you stirring up? Your mother? She's not a guest."

Rachel sits up straighter. She's going to tell him something; he's not going to like it. "Sometimes, Grandpa, you could thank her for the things she does for you."

"Thank her? For what?"

"Ma is always doing things for you. Always! Didn't she cut your hair last week? She does thousands of things for you."

He pops his bridge out of his mouth, then shoves it back in. "She's family," he says, as if that explains everything.

Rachel could argue the point, but she doesn't have the heart for it. With every word Izzy says, she hears the engine of his lungs.

"You're a troublemaker," he says, but he's benign in his victory. "How do you like my eggs?"

"Very good."

"Add a little water, that's the secret. Eva always liked my scrambled eggs." He pauses, fork in the air. "There were times, though . . . she wouldn't eat anything I made."

"Why?"

"She got mad at me. Wouldn't talk to me, wouldn't even look at me."

"You probably didn't thank her for anything, either."

"I was never easy to live with."

149

"You could have fooled me."

He looks across the table at her. There's a little smile in the corner of his mouth.

Rachel eats everything in sight, but Izzy doesn't even finish the small amount of egg on his plate. "Grandpa, you didn't eat much. You hardly tasted the spaghetti."

He passes his hand in a familiar gesture over his chest. "It's this . . . cough. I don't have that much appetite." He leans across the table toward her. "What did the doctor say?"

Rachel's heart jumps. "Who?" Her mother is right. He's lost weight. She sees now how angular and thin his face has become.

"The doctor. The boy doctor with the mouth like this." He puts his fingers at the side of his mouth and pushes up his lips.

She's too scared to laugh. "You mean Dr. North?"

"Who else? Don't you know anything? Eh! Why should I ask you?"

Her face flushes. "What do you want to know?"

"I want to know what you know." He speaks distinctly and without any pauses. "I want to know what he said. He talked to Shirley, didn't he?"

How does he know that? His eyes remain fixed on her and she sees, as if suddenly enlarged, the waxy-looking lids, the pale eyelashes. "Grandpa," she stammers. "Yes, but . . . what—what do you want me to say?"

"The truth," he says after a moment. "What did the doctor say about me?"

She tries to think. What should she say? How much? How little? She can't lie. Doesn't know what the lie would be. Wouldn't, anyway. Couldn't, not to

150

Izzy. She crumples her napkin, scrubs a little spot on the table. "Grandpa—"

"How sick am I?"

"Pretty—pretty sick, Grandpa."

"It's this virus, huh?"

"Well . . ."

"It's more than the virus?"

She nods.

"How much more?"

"Quite a bit. It's—it's not too good."

"They have a name for it?"

She nods again.

"You know what it is?"

"Yes."

He waits. She doesn't say anything, keeps scrubbing at that little spot.

"What is it, Rachel? What do they call it?"

The calmness of his voice reassures her. She looks at him, starts to speak, then pushes back her chair and rushes into the kitchen. She looks around. A large worn spot on the floor right in front of the stove catches her eye. She wonders how often Izzy has stood in that exact spot cooking an egg or making himself a hamburger. What did she come in here for? She had something in her mind, but she can't remember. She turns on the faucet, runs the cold water. "You want a glass of water, Grandpa?" she calls.

"No."

She drinks the water slowly. Her nose becomes clogged. Is she going to cry? She blows her nose on a napkin, goes back into the other room. She will be as calm as he is. She sits down at the table. "Grandpa, maybe you should ask Ma."

"Maybe I should, but I'm asking you."

She presses her lips together and half smiles.

"Are you going to tell me, Rachel?"

She's still got that crooked half smile. "If you want me to."

"I want you to."

"Grandpa, it's called—"

"Yes?" he says. "Yes?" And there's an eager look on his face, young, boyish, as if he's waiting to hear good news.

"Mesothelioma," she says. Her heart is going at a sickening rate.

"Mesothelioma," he repeats. "What's that?"

She tells him. She tells him whatever he wants to know. When she's done, she sits there and cries, and he pats her hand.

TWENTY-EIGHT

"Today, we're taking a little bus trip," Izzy says, and he won't answer any questions. "You'll see," he says. That's all. They wait at the bus stop. It's Saturday afternoon, and there's a small crowd of people. Izzy climbs on the bus slowly, gets out his money slowly, that's the way he does everything now, slowly takes a seat in front.

Rachel sits down next to him. "Ready to tell me where we're going?"

"Wait and see."

"What's the mystery? Why won't you tell me?"

"Don't ask so many questions."

They get off on Richardson Avenue on the west side of the city, an old, half-ruined street stuck between the interstate highway and the university. Izzy leads the way past big, old square houses with lines of washing strung across the porches. They pass boarded-up stores, an empty lot littered with rubble and papers, a bar with a blue neon sign, a small, dank-looking factory.

They turn on West Creek Street. The street is divided by Clearbrook Creek, one lane on one side, one lane on the other. At Fullmer Avenue, the first cross street, the creek flows under a small, arched bridge. He stands on the bridge, looking down the embankment. Its steeply sloping sides are overgrown with sumac and knotweed. Now Rachel gets her first glimmer of what's going on. "Grandpa, did you build this bridge?"

"Chsss. Chsss." Izzy holds up his hand, silences her. He examines the wall on one side, then crosses to the other side and does the same thing.

"What are you looking for?"

"Chsss. Chssss."

They walk down West Creek Street until the next cross street, where there's another bridge. This time Izzy goes cautiously down the embankment so he can take a closer look at the wall. He does this on both sides of the bridge. All along West Creek Street, the creek is bridged, and at each bridge, Izzy stops, scrambles slowly sideways down the embankment and examines the walls.

Rachel is afraid he'll slip and follows him, staying close. He's getting short-winded and tired. "Why can't you tell me what's going on? Can't I do something to help you?"

"No." He won't say anything else. It's not until they're on the bus again, going home, that he remarks, "I worked on every one of those bridges."

"I know that, Grandpa. You told me."

"Well, you don't know everything. You don't know I left something there, on one of them, do you? Left my handprint." A little smile crosses his face. "Put my hand into the wet cement. One of those bridges . . . I don't remember which one. I used to know." He looks out the window. He's silent for a long time. Then he says, "Five fingers in the mud and my initials. I. S."

"Lewis, if you were going to leave your mark, what would it be?" Rachel says. "If you could do

154

one thing you knew was going to be around years later, something that said, 'Lewis was here . . .' "

He leans back in the booth. "It could be anything?" They're in Poppie's diner again, before Rachel goes to work.

"Anything signifying you."

"The essential me? A flapping mouth."

"You don't talk that much. Do you think you talk a lot?"

"To you I do."

"Yes, but sometimes, Lewis, when we're with Helena and Mikey, you don't say a word."

" 'Cause I'm looo-ooking at yooo-oooou," he sings, and he catches Rachel's hand under the table.

Poppie comes over with their order. Rice pudding in big blue bowls. "This is great," Lewis says to Poppie. His hands are now folded on the table.

"Just made it fresh."

Rachel tells Lewis about her expedition with Izzy. "We went all up and down the street, we probably looked at every bridge—ten of them, at least. You know what I think, Lewis? I think he left his handprint the way an artist signs a painting."

"You mean, 'This is my work and I'm proud of it'? Good theory. . . . Are you going to finish your rice pudding?"

She takes another spoonful, shoves the bowl over to him. "I think it's more than a theory. I mean, it *is* a theory. I can't prove it, but I really believe it."

"Why don't you ask your grandfather why he did it?"

"If you knew him, Lewis—"

"Sometimes I think I do, you talk about him so much."

"You can *ask* Izzy things, but Izzy only tells you what Izzy wants to tell you."

* * *

"Let's stop someplace, Grandpa," Rachel says. They're out, it's cold today, and Izzy's face is suddenly covered with sweat. "I've got my pay in my pocket. I'll treat you to an ice cream."

"Too cold for ice cream."

"Okay, I'll treat you to a sandwich."

"I'm not hungry."

She takes another look at him. His lips are pale, trembling with the effort of breathing. "Grandpa, *I'd* like to stop."

They go into a little coffee shop and sit down at a table near the window. "Hello, folks." The waitress drops a menu on the table. "What will it be?"

Rachel picks up the menu, studies it. "Order," Izzy says. His head is back, he's still breathing hard. "Order . . . something." His voice is irritable. "Can't sit here and . . . make . . . her wait. Busy . . . woman."

Rachel orders a sandwich and ice cream. "What about you, Grandpa?"

"Nothing. . . ."

"Grandpa, I'm treating. Have a sandwich." She points to the menu. "Doesn't this one look good?"

It occurs to Rachel that she sounds an awful lot like her mother, who's constantly trying to get Izzy to eat more. Shirley is disturbed by his loss of weight, and on Sundays, when they're all together, she keeps up a running patter about food, urging him to eat the little delicacies she's fixed for him.

And now he says, just as on Sunday, "I have no appetite."

"Have some ice cream, then. Who needs an appetite to eat ice cream?" Rachel argues. Meanwhile, the waitress is standing patiently by the table with her pad in hand.

156

"We don't want to keep this lady . . . waiting, Rachel."

"That's perfectly all right," the waitress says. She's got tight black hair covered with a net. "If you want ice cream, we make our own, fresh every day. Strawberry's my favorite."

"Maple walnut is what I like," Izzy says.

"Oh, our maple walnut is grand. Real walnuts."

"Try it, Grandpa. I'll share it with you."

The ice cream comes. Izzy eats it slowly but he eats it all. Rachel can't wait to get home and tell her mother that Izzy ate a whole dish of ice cream. All those good, rich calories.

"Well, I enjoyed that," he admits when they leave.

"Me, too. We'll go back there."

"Maybe."

"No, we will," she says. She wants him to agree. She wants him to say, yes, they will go back there and eat maple-walnut ice cream, maybe next week, maybe the week after. Maybe next month. She wants him to say, yes, they have time—and time—and time.

But over the next few days, she notices how much harder it is for him to breathe. Each day, it's harder for him to breathe than it was the day before.

Sometimes, at night especially, just before she falls asleep, Rachel thinks—she *tries* to think—about Izzy dying. Always the question arises: What does it mean that he's dying? He's alive. How can he be dying. She says it softly, aloud. "Dying." Then louder. "Dying." She says it over and over until the word becomes senseless, nothing but a collection of letters stripped of meaning. Dyingdyingdyingdying dying . . . dyng dyng dyng dyng. . . .

But at other times, also at night, always at night, it

157

comes to her differently. *He's dying.* Just like that. *Yes, it's going to happen.* The voice is calm, authoritative. She rebels against it with a flash of anger and temper. She is only now getting to know her grandfather. It's out of the question for him to die!

The voice reminds her that she has nothing to do with this. This is not something she can control. A temper tantrum supreme, one of her best displays, will make no difference, will change nothing.

Dying. Dying. The moment when she almost caught the truth of it, the sense of it, was that evening Izzy questioned her, when she had to name his disease to him and tell him what it meant. And felt herself falling into a space where she had never been before, falling as if down a chute or through a vast, featureless, airless tunnel.

She sits up in bed, hugs her pillow to her. She remembers Dr. North saying he wasn't, could never be, "one hundred percent sure" of his diagnosis. *There,* she thinks, as if vindicated. Maybe her grandfather is thin, maybe he walks slowly and wheezes, but so what? Lots of people are thin and short of breath, and they're not all dying.

TWENTY-NINE

Saturday. Today, when we stopped to rest, Grandpa started talking again about the handprint he left in the wet cement. "When my boss—Dondahough was his name, we used to call him Dandy because he changed his shirt twice a day—when he found out what I had done, he fired me."

"For that? For a little thing like that? Why would he want to lose a good worker like you?"

"Those were the days of the big depression. Men were waiting in line for my job. A line around the block and all the way to the next city. Those days, one wrong step and you hit the bricks. You don't know," he told me.

He's always telling me that. *You don't know.* Maybe I don't, but I thought it was awful that he got fired and I said so. "Nobody could even see that handprint, could they?"

"Dandy could. The man had sharp eyes. Well, he was right. I shouldn't have done it."

"No, I don't think he was right. I don't agree, Grandpa, I don't agree at all."

"I suppose if it was you, you would have argued with him?"

159

"Yes. If I was right. Didn't you?"

"At the time, I did."

"And so?"

"I was wrong. What if every man on the job put his hand in the cement?"

He had me there. I had to admit that could be a problem.

That was all he wanted. For me to see the light, to see that what he was saying was right. I wanted to know more. Did he get another job right away? I could have asked him two dozen questions, but he was through talking.

Tuesday. Sitting around talking to Grandpa yesterday, he said, "Your mother should have named you for my Eva."

"Why?"

"It was not a respectful thing. She should have named you after her own mother. To show respect."

"I'm named after my other grandmother. Daddy's mother."

"Why do you tell me things I know?" he demanded.

What a face he had! What a voice! For a moment, all I wanted to do was get away from him, get away from that face and that voice. It was like a storm passing over me. Then it was gone, I was calm again. "Grandpa, look at it this way. Maybe in another life my name will be Eva."

He didn't think that was the least bit funny. But all this made me think of something—that I'm not scared of Grandpa. I should say, not scared anymore, because now that I think about it, I was before.

* * *

Friday. I thought I had all the dogs cased on the streets Grandpa and I walk, but I got a surprise on Blake Avenue. A big white dog ran out from behind a house, snarling as if it owned the world. I try not to act cowardly around dogs, but I was off-guard, taken by surprise, and I cried out. Grandpa put his arm over my shoulder. "Just keep walking." Even after we were past the dog, he kept his arm around my shoulder.

THIRTY

It's drizzling outside. Izzy's chest is bothering him. "Tight," he says, putting his hand on his breastbone. And he coughs and coughs and coughs. They decide to stay in. Izzy lies on the couch, his legs covered with a blanket.

"Not a very good day for Scrabble, is it?" Rachel says.

"Go home. You don't have to stay."

"I'll hang around for a while."

"It's boring."

"For you?" she says.

"For you!"

"Not for me, Grandpa. I'm fine. Look at me, I'm happy as a bug in a rug." She's sitting back in his chair, eating an apple, her feet up on the magazine table. "You know what I'd like, though? I'd like to see your pictures."

"What pictures?"

"Snapshots. Photographs. Do you have any albums?"

"What do you want with pictures?"

No matter what she says, he always has to resist. It's like a code of honor. Or maybe it's just habit and he can't help it. "I'd like to see you when you were young."

"Nobody took my picture."

"Why not? I bet you were cute."

"I didn't like it." The blanket rises and falls with the rise and fall of his chest. "I never liked having my picture taken."

"How about Grandma Eva?"

"Oh, her." He sits up, pushes the blanket off impatiently. "She liked it. Hold up a camera . . . and she stood right up and . . . smiled."

"So you have pictures of her. Where are they?"

"What for? You know what she looks like."

"True." Her mother has pictures of Grandma Eva in their albums at home. "But maybe you have some different ones. You probably do."

"Pictures," he says breathily. "What use . . . are pictures? Take a picture. Smile. Look happy. Everybody always wants to take a picture."

"It's so you can remember things. It helps you remember. If you didn't have pictures of Grandma, how would I know what she looked like?"

"What difference does it make?"

"It makes a difference to me." Rachel is enjoying this verbal boxing match. She used to give up when Izzy got that brusque, argumentative tone of voice. Now she just keeps going. "Where have you got them hidden, Grandpa? I know you have pictures someplace. Are they in your bedroom? I'll go get them."

"You don't have to get . . . things in my house." He gets up and goes into the other room. He opens a bureau drawer, pulling it out as if it's extremely heavy, then slowly pushes aside clothes, linens, various things wrapped in plastic bags. He closes the drawer, puffing, then struggles with the middle drawer.

"Grandpa, can I do that?" She knows he's weaker, has less strength for walking, but it never occurred to her that opening a bureau drawer could be so difficult.

In the bottom drawer, he finds a manila envelope stuffed with pictures.

Rachel sits down on the bed next to Izzy. The pictures are brownish, the paper has gone soft with age. Izzy pushes aside pictures of men in fedoras and women in mid-calf-length dresses.

"Who are they?" Rachel says.

"Just people."

"Friends of yours and Grandma's?"

"It's nothing. They're all dead."

"Wait. Let me see these." She takes her time over snapshots of him and her grandmother. "Grandpa, what a handsome devil! And Grandma was beautiful, you're right."

There are pictures she's never seen before. One, she likes especially. Eva, perhaps fourteen or fifteen years old, standing on the roof peak of a house, wearing a dress with a big lace collar, hands on her hips, and looking into the camera, straight into it, with a glint of a smile.

Rachel can't stop looking at the picture. This was her grandmother, this girl, this young person, this serious and smiling young woman. "I wish I'd known her."

"You want this picture?"

"Oh, yes! But don't you want it?"

"It's for you."

"Thank you." She kisses him.

He lies back on the pillow and talks about his family, his parents, his older brother, his three sisters. "My father came here first ... with his father, from Poland. He met my mother here. They were poor, nobody had time for things like playing. You grew up fast. When I was ... thirteen, I was a man already. ..." He closes his eyes, opens them a moment later. "She sang. My mother. She would sit at the table and drink tea ... and sing."

He falls asleep. Rachel sits there and looks at the pictures. Suddenly Izzy wakes up and says, "I built her a house."

"Who? Your mother?"

"Eva. You ask your mother. That's where she grew up ... for a while—in the house I built. A brick ... house. Built it myself." He sits up, becomes animated. "I don't mean I hired somebody. I hear these people talking. ... *I* did this, *I* did that. They didn't do it, they just paid ... for it. We had to sell it. Some problems about ... money." He puts his hand to his chest, as if to hold in his breath, save it, preserve it.

"Eva said, 'We're going to sell the house ... don't worry, it's going to be all right.' She was ... very practical about money." He stops, breathes, takes out his handkerchief, coughs into it. "I always gave her my paycheck, every week."

Rachel thinks about her grandmother, who stood on a roof when she was fifteen and got married when she was seventeen. How did she learn to be practical about money? "Where'd you meet Eva, Grandpa?"

"Ahhh! Who remembers?" he says, and remembers. "I met her on a beach."

"What beach?"

"What does that matter? Fairview, Lake Ontario. She was coming out of the water, all wet ... and I saw her and I said to my friend ... who was with me, 'Look at that girl. Now that's what I call ... a beautiful girl.'" His eyes open as if he's looking through a window. "And when she walked by me, I looked right at her, very bold. I was bold in some ways but very quiet, backward ... in other ways. I didn't know how to talk, how to . . . start up with a girl. So . . ." He wipes his mouth, sinks back against the pillow, breathes.

"I kept going to the beach. . . . Every Saturday I went and hoped I would meet her. She was always there, she was a wonderful swimmer. . . . I would go in swimming and hope to meet her . . . in the water."

"Did you? What happened?"

"What happened? One day, she's not swimming, she's running on the beach . . . so, just like that, I don't know what came over me . . . I got up and started running with her." He's tired. His voice is hoarse. His breath is raspy. "From there, everything happened. The whole story. . . . We got to know each other."

A few times a week now, Rachel stays and eats supper with Izzy. She cooks hamburgers, boils potatoes, throws a piece of steak down onto the frying pan. "Does it smell good, Grandpa?" She can't cook the way her mother does, but she can usually get him to eat a little. Later, Manny and Shirley come over to pick her up, but first they sit around and talk to Izzy for a while. Sometimes they stay for an hour or two, watching TV with him while Rachel does her homework.

Tonight, though, Lewis is coming over. "We're going to a basketball game, Grandpa."

"Mmm-huh." He walks slowly into the kitchen, slowly washes off his plate.

"He wants to meet you." Rachel dries the dishes, puts them away.

"Mmm-huh."

When the door bell rings, she and Izzy are in the living room, watching TV. "I'll get it." She jumps up. "Grandpa, do I look okay?"

He glances at her, shrugs.

Lewis is wearing white sneakers and a long overcoat. There's a fragrant odor of shampoo and soap coming from him.

She squeezes his fingers. "Come meet my grandfather."

He follows her in and she makes the introductions. "Lewis, this is my grandfather, Mr. Shapiro." Hand extended, Lewis bends over Izzy, who didn't get up to greet him—but that's okay, Rachel thinks quickly, he's old, he's sick. "Grandpa, this is Lewis Oliver Olswanger." Why did she throw in Lewis's middle name? It sounds pretentious. Izzy picks right up on it.

"So your name is Lewis . . . Oliver . . . Ol . . . swanger?"

Rachel stares at her grandfather. He did that on purpose, dragging out Lewis's name, making it sound silly.

"What kind of a name is that?"

"Lewis. Just Lewis is what they call me, Mr. Shapiro." He is still standing there with his hand out, waiting to shake Izzy's hand.

Izzy takes Lewis's hand, Lewis's clean, thin, long-fingered hand, in his own broad, grainy palm, but he doesn't shake. He turns Lewis's hand over and over, examines it like some kind of foreign matter.

Rachel watches this, transfixed. She knows Izzy, she knows something is coming, something she's probably not going to like.

"No strength in this hand," Izzy says. "You couldn't be a stonemason . . . with hands like this." His breath whistles in his chest. He drops Lewis's hand; discards it, really.

Lewis doesn't look at Rachel, his face is flushed, his ears are blazing. Her own face is hot and her stomach is lurching. She looks from one to the other. She wants to defend Lewis to Izzy—*Grandpa, give him a chance, you'd like him*—and just as much she wants to defend Izzy to Lewis—*don't think he's like this all the time, Lewis, he's really nice underneath.*

"Well, go on," Izzy says. He reaches out to change the channel. "Go on, Rachel. You're going out, aren't you?"

Rachel gets her jacket. "Good-bye, Grandpa. See you tomorrow."

He waves dismissively, doesn't look up from the TV.

"I thought," Lewis says as they are going down the stairs, "from all the things you've said about him that he was this great old man."

"Well, he is," Rachel says quickly.

"Yeah? You mean he's not always like that?"

"Like what?" Rachel says, as if she doesn't know exactly what Lewis means.

"Rough," Lewis says. "Is he always as rough as that?"

"He doesn't have smooth edges. He's not a slick guy."

"I feel sorry for you, Rachel, stuck with him every day."

"Save it, Lewis. Nobody's forcing me." Her words are okay, but her tone is curt.

He shrugs and grins and strides along and doesn't say anything else.

"Lewis?"

"Yeah?"

"Hold on a minute, you're walking too fast."

He shrugs again but slows down.

"I'm sorry about that."

"It doesn't matter."

168

"It does. That ridiculous thing with your hands—"

"I don't know . . ." Lewis holds up his hands. "He's right, isn't he? I couldn't be a stonemason."

"Do you want to be a stonemason?"

"Not the last time I thought about it."

"I didn't mean to snap at you."

"It's okay."

"Are you still mad at me?"

Lewis shakes his head.

"Are you sure?"

"Pretty sure."

"You *are* mad at me."

"I'm not."

"Yes, you are. Wait a second." She reaches up and kisses him. "Well . . . ?"

"Still mad," he mumbles against her lips. "You gotta try harder."

"Oh, he didn't," Shirley says to Rachel the next morning. "Did he really? Manny, did you hear this?" she calls to Rachel's father.

From the living-room couch, where he's reclining in his stocking feet, conducting *H.M.S. Pinafore,* Manny calls back, "What? I can't hear you."

Rachel follows her mother into the living room.

" 'I'm called Little Buttercup—dear little Buttercup . . .' " Her father's large, pudgy hands rise and fall with the notes. Flash of gold ring. The record spins, the needle hops, Buttercup is suddenly a step ahead of the great conductor.

"I like Tony Martin, myself," Shirley says, turning down the music, and she tells Manny about Izzy's examining Lewis's hands.

When her mother was listening to Rachel a few moments ago, she had a serious, understanding expression. She nodded her head, pursed her lips disapprovingly. But now, telling Manny the same thing she's just heard from Rachel, she starts laughing. "My father's so impossible." And Manny laughs, too, his face creasing up like a pudding.

"It's not really funny, you guys," Rachels says from the doorway.

"You're right, darling," Manny says. "Anyway, I'm sure he didn't mean anything by it."

"Daddy, Grandpa was being mean. I saw it on his face. I couldn't believe it was happening. He just met Lewis for the first time, and he was definitely being killer mean."

"No, no, you've got to understand, Izzy's whole life was spent working with his hands. Naturally, he judges other people the same way."

"Manny, he did the same thing to you," Shirley says.

"Looked at my hands? No, he didn't."

"Oh, yes. All my boyfriends, he did it to them all, every one. And you—he gave you such a hard time. That's why we sneaked away to be married. You were so mad at him."

"I wasn't mad at your father. I always liked your father."

"I never knew you sneaked away to be married," Rachel says.

"And then Mama was so upset that we got married by a justice of the peace that we—"

Manny sits up. "Shirl, from the moment I met your father—"

"We got married again, with a rabbi. Now, you remember that, don't you, Manny?"

"Right from the beginning, I liked your father."

"No, now, Manny, you didn't like him that first year."

170

"This is not true, sweetheart. I saw his good qualities. And your mother, I loved your mother."

"Yes, but we're not talking about Mama. You're rewriting history."

Rachel's head goes back and forth, as if she's at a tennis match. It's a parents' match.

"Manny, my father, when you first met him, he literally terrified you. Remember what you said to me?"

"Shirl—"

"My memory is crystal clear on this point."

"Shirl, I am absolutely positive—"

The argument continues, but Rachel isn't following it. It's just come to her why Izzy was so rude to Lewis. He was jealous. Jealous of her.

THIRTY-ONE

Tuesday. Grandpa fell again. We were walking and suddenly he grabbed my arm, dragged at me so hard, I was sure we were both going down. He was breathing like this: Uhhhh! . . . uhhhh! . . . uhhhhh! Fast and sort of panicky, as if it were just impossible for him to get his breath.

It was just luck that we were near a bus stop. We sat down on the bench. We must have sat there for at least an hour. And then we took a bus home.

I didn't tell Ma and Daddy what happened. It's stupid of me, but I knew Ma would get really upset and want to run off to the doctor with Grandpa. I thought, What for? I haven't forgotten what the doctor said that day in his office. *There's nothing to do.* Nothing, except to make Grandpa feel as good as possible.

But there's another reason I didn't want to tell Ma. I'm just realizing it now as I'm writing. I don't know how to say this exactly, but maybe it's as if, by not telling, I'm protecting Grandpa. From what? From knowing what he already knows?

Or does he know? I remember that the day he questioned me about his disease, the one question

172

he didn't ask was the most basic one. He never said, in so many words, "Am I going to die?" And I never said it in so many words. I couldn't. I just couldn't come out and say it.

And since then—I see it now—I've let myself slip into the thought or the wish that none of it is true.

In a way, we're all doing it, we're all making believe—Ma, Daddy, and me—because we never really talk about it. We talk about him being *sick,* or *tired,* or *losing weight.* We're all thinking about the other thing, but we don't say it. And when Grandpa fell, it must have gone through my mind that if I didn't talk about his falling, it would be almost as if it hadn't happened. I didn't reason it out; it was a feeling that went through me. Almost an instinct. Pretend everything's okay. Even while we sat on the bench at the bus stop and I was terrified for him, I said, "How do you feel now, Grandpa?" And then I chatted him up as if nothing was wrong.

Wednesday. I told Ma what happened. I knew she'd be upset that I hadn't told her right away. I tried to explain, but she didn't understand my reasons. "I depend on you," she said. "You've been so good. You've been wonderful. I don't know what I would have done all this time without you going to Grandpa every day."

"Ma, I didn't let you down."

"You should have told me right away, Rachel. That was irresponsible."

"I'm sorry! Okay? How many times do I have to say it?"

She stared at me hard. "Why don't you start cleaning up here? I'm going to call the doctor."

I ran water in the sink, listened to her talk to Dr. North.

When she hung up, she just stood there.

"What'd he say?"

She got a dish towel, pulled a plate out of the rack, and started drying it. "He said it's a sign the disease is progessing. He said we should watch Izzy carefully and we should call him anytime."

"Did he want to see Grandpa?"

She kept drying the plate, rubbing the towel round and round and round it. "No."

"Did he say anything else?"

"No." Still drying the same plate. "The way he talks, it doesn't make any difference if we called him today, or yesterday, or the day after tomorrow."

I dumped silverware into the rack. "Ma, that plate is dry."

She looked at the plate. "What? Oh." She put it down, picked up another plate, then put it back and said, "Rachey, I'm sorry I yelled at you. I shouldn't have."

"Ma, it's okay."

"No, I was just so upset about Grandpa—"

"I know. It's okay. Really." I meant it, but when I went upstairs to my room, I was suddenly so angry, I wanted to punch something. Not angry at Ma, exactly. More angry at the doctor, at the world, at *something*. I kicked my sneakers across the room. *The disease is progressing.* I tore the spread off my bed, threw it on the floor, tore my bed apart. Then I flung myself down, I wanted to cry, I wanted to, but I couldn't.

THIRTY-TWO

"It's my birthday tomorrow," Helena says as they meet in the hall between classes.

"I forgot it! Helena, I didn't even get you a present," Rachel says. "Some friend I am."

"Yeah, you're rotten. I want you and Lewis to come over after school tomorrow and have cake and stuff with me and Mikey."

"Helena, I'm going to my grandfather's."

"Can't you miss one day with your grandfather? Would it make that much difference? We hardly see)ou at all anymore, Rachel."

Rachel thinks of the near fall Izzy had, of his fatigue yesterday. "I shouldn't," she says softly.

"It'll be no fun without you. Did I tell you Mikey's making the cake?"

"I didn't know he could bake."

"I didn't, either, but he said, trust me, so what could I do?"

"Why don't we all party tomorrow night?"

"Mom and Dad are taking me out to The Garden Café."

"I'm sorry." Rachel puts her arm around Helena. "Have a good party without me."

"I don't want to have a good party without you. I want you there."

"I'm sorry," Rachel says again. What else can she say?

Friday, it's cloudy when she and Izzy go out for their walk. He seems a little slower, perhaps puts his feet down a little more carefully, but otherwise, as far as Rachel can tell, he's all right. It begins to rain lightly as they pass the soccer field, and they debate walking back or taking shelter. Rachel's for taking shelter, Izzy's for walking back. "What's a little water?" They walk back.

Helena, Mikey, and Lewis are waiting for them in front of Izzy's apartment. Lewis has a bunch of balloons tied to his wrist.

"You guys—I don't believe this," Rachel says.

"We brought my party to you." Helena has the ice cream. Mikey has the cake.

Lewis flaps his fingers hello to Rachel, looks sideways at Izzy.

"What is this?" Izzy says, and they all start explaining.

"Grandpa, it's Helena's—"

"—my best friend, I didn't want to have a birthday party without her."

"—and we just thought, Mr. Shapiro . . ."

But finally, it's Helena who takes Izzy's hand, Helena who says, "Mr. Shapiro, my grandfather lives in Cincinnati. I thought you could be sort of a substitute for him today."

Rachel smiles, claps her hand to her forehead. That kind of stuff is not going to work on Izzy. So she thinks. But before she can say mean man, Izzy is unlocking the door and holding it open, and they're all pouring in. *Thud, thud, thud,* the floor shakes under their feet. Mikey turns on the radio, Helena cuts the cake, Lewis sticks balloons on the walls.

Rachel pushes aside a balloon that drifts onto her

head, turns down the radio. It's too noisy, it's too frantic, it's too much for Izzy. His hands were shaking as he unlocked the door. Now he's sitting in his chair, looking frail and gray.

"Let's have some of this fantastic cake," Mikey says, unwrapping the paper plates. "Where're the candles, Helena?"

"Wait," she says. "Mr. Shapiro, when's your birthday?"

"What for?" He's sitting a little forward, frowning.

"We should celebrate your birthday, too. Happy birthday to you and me at the same time."

"You couldn't get enough candles for how old I am. If I meet somebody on the street, they say, 'Shapiro? You look great. . . . I thought you were dead.' "

Rachel catches Lewis's eye, and he winks, as if to say, Well, what can I say, you were right about him. He is great.

"Give Mr. Shapiro three candles, Mikey," Lewis says. "One for good luck. One for good behavior. And one to grow on."

Mikey lights the candles on the cake. "Come on, everybody, sing." And he starts. "Happy birthday to you, happy birthday, dear Helena . . ."

Rachel looks around at her friends, at Mikey's blond, straight hair, at Helena's round and pretty cat face, at Lewis's ears, all flushed and shining with light. Izzy is singing, too, and Rachel begins to relax.

"Now we sing to you, Grandpa," Helena says. "Is it all right if I call you Grandpa?" She's kneeling in front of Izzy, and she stays right there while they all sing to him.

And, oh, this is terrible, but Rachel is jealous. She hates hearing Helena call Izzy Grandpa, feels as if her friend is taking something away from her. Worse yet, she can see that Izzy doesn't mind at all. His feet are bouncing like a boy's.

They eat ice cream and Mikey's cake, which is not fantastic, but is very good. Rachel and Lewis sit on the floor next to each other. "Whose idea was this?" she says.

"Helena's. Who else? How about this cake? My cousin's got talent."

"I almost fell over when I saw you guys at the door."

Helena gets up and takes Mikey's hand. "Now we've got to work off all this cake. Come on, you two," she says to Rachel and Lewis. "Up! We're going to dance." They push the chairs and the rug aside.

"Wild dancing," Izzy says. The floor shakes, the windows rattle, they're all sweating and laughing. Helena switches to a soft-music station and holds out her hands to Izzy. "Mr. Shapiro—Grandpa. The birthday boy has to dance."

Izzy gets to his feet, puts one hand lightly on Helena's waist. "And a one and a two, and away we go," he says. "Clap the rhythm, Olswatter." Mangling Lewis's name makes everyone laugh again, and Izzy lets go of Helena, wriggles his hips, raises his hands, starts dancing as if he's somebody sixty years younger.

"You're wonderful," Helena says. "Were you always such a terrific dancer?"

"I liked it as well . . . as the next man." Izzy's hoarse, his breath is coming in puffs, but he's smiling, his cheeks are bright with heat. "I was strong . . . it was nothing after a day's work . . . for me to take Eva dancing. Dance all night and . . . go to work . . . the next day."

He stops dancing, getting his breath, but holds the floor. "I used to pick up my wife with one hand . . . put my hand on the floor . . ." He bends over, demonstrating. "Like this. She'd stand on it and . . . I'd raise her. Pick her up . . . straight up in the air. . . ."

"One hand?" Helena says. "That's amazing."

"I'm still pretty strong." Izzy nods around at the little circle of faces.

"I bet you are," Mikey says politely. Izzy puts his hands around Helena's waist as if to lift her. "Way to go," Mikey says, and they all laugh and stir around.

But Izzy's not pretending. He's trying to lift Helena. He wants to lift her off the floor, into the air. Rachel turns her head away, she doesn't look, she doesn't want to see this. Pick up Helena? That big, solid girl? She must weigh almost as much as Izzy does. He can't pick her up. He can't do it. It's absurd, it's terrible, and in a moment, it's frightening.

"Uhhh . . ." He's puffing, he's got his hands around Helena's waist, he's straining to lift her. Everyone has gone quiet. Sweat pops out on Izzy's forehead; his face lengthens, tightens. His breath starts coming like a bellows. *"Huuuu . . . huuuu . . . huuuu . . ."*

"Grandpa," Rachel says. "Grandpa! Stop."

Helena looks frantically at Rachel; she's on her toes, trying to help him.

"Huuuu . . . huuuu . . . huuuu . . ." There's no other sound in the room, only that agonized pull of breath. Izzy's face is gray, sweating, he's got Helena in the air . . . for a second, for two seconds, for three. He sets her down with a thump. "You . . . see," he says. He smiles all around, a strange, blind smile. He sits down on the couch, that blind smile frozen on his face. He sees Lewis standing by the window and

179

in a voice barely audible, he says, "Olswatter. *Huuuu . . . huuuu . . . huuuu . . .* Sit . . . down, Olswatter. . . . You didn't . . . sit down . . . *huuuu . . . huuuu . . . huuuu . . .* once."

"That's okay—" Lewis begins.

But Rachel grabs his arm and says, "Lewis. Sit down." And he sits down.

"Mr. Shapiro," Mikey says in a frightened voice, "can I get you something?" He looks at Rachel. "Should I get him a drink of water?"

"Don't make . . . a . . . fuss. . . ." Izzy's head falls back, his eyes close. *"Huuuu . . . huuuu . . . huuuu . . ."*

"Rache," Helena whispers. A silence closes over them all.

"You better go," Rachel says.

Obediently, they gather up the remains of the cake, pull on their jackets, and tiptoe to the door. Rachel wets a washcloth and wipes Izzy's face. His eyes flutter open.

She covers him with a blanket and cleans up the mess in the room. Then she sits down near him. She listens to his breathing. She sits there for a long time. Outside, it's dark.

When he wakes up, he says, "Still here? Go home . . . darling."

THIRTY-THREE

When Rachel arrives at Izzy's apartment on Saturday morning, he is sitting on the couch, wearing an undershirt. She notices how thin his arms are, thin and smooth. He is sitting completely still, he only glances up when she enters. She sits down next to him, links her arm through his. "Grandpa? How are you?"

"How should I be?"

"Everybody was worried about you."

"Who is this everybody?"

"Are you kidding, Grandpa? *Everybody.*" Last night, Helena had called, then Lewis, both of them anxious and feeling guilty. "Ma, me, and Daddy aside, I'm talking about my friends. They all called. They were all worried."

"Oh, your friends. The wild dancers."

"Did you know Mikey made that cake?"

"He's a baker?"

"No, he's going to be a pilot. He takes flying lessons."

"What about the skinny one? What can he do?"

"Lewis? A lot of things. He's very nice."

"Mmm-huh."

Okay, she thinks, *that's enough about Lewis. Let's not get into that this morning.* "Grandpa, did you sleep on the couch?"

"I never left it."

"Was it comfortable?"

He nods. It's remarkable, but he doesn't look particularly tired this morning. "You're here early," he says.

"Oh, am I?" She pretends innocence. In fact, she's been dressed and waiting to come here for hours. Very early in the morning, before it was even light, she had gone downstairs to the kitchen, picked up the phone, and dialed his number. She wanted to hear his voice, she wanted to hear him say, "Stop worrying! I'm okay. What's all the fuss about?" Before his phone could ring, she came to her senses and hung up.

"I wanted to call you last night, but it was too late."

"Last night," he says, "I saw Eva."

Rachel looks at him quickly. "You dreamed about Grandma?"

He is having none of that. "I saw her. She was here and I saw her. She told me, 'Izzy, you're an old fool.' "

"Well, Grandpa, why would she say that?"

"If you don't know, you're a young fool."

Rachel bends her head in acknowledgment. *Touché.* "Kind of a strenuous day," she says. "How do you feel this morning, Grandpa?"

He gives her a little smile. "Like an old fool." He gets up, shuffles into the bathroom, the whispery sound of his breath, *huuu . . . huuu . . . huuu . . . ,* moving with him. She hears water running, the flush of the toilet. When he comes back, she smells toothpaste and soap, his hair is combed, he's put on a green shirt, and a tie is looped around his collar.

"I've never seen you wear a tie, Grandpa."

"No?" He stands in front of the mirror, knotting the tie with fingers that shake slightly. He finishes the knot, smoothes down the tie, smoothes down his hair.

In the kitchen, he puts a slice of bread in the toaster, fries an egg in butter. "Did you eat breakfast?"

"No, not really."

"You want something? I'll fry an egg for you."

"Egg in the morning?" She makes a face. "No thanks, Grandpa."

He carries his food to the table and sits down. He forks egg onto toast, takes a bite, and puts it down. "The sun is shining." He pushes aside his plate. "I want to stay out all day. What time is it?"

She looks at her watch. "Eight-thirty."

"It's late. Let's go." He gets up, puts on his jacket.

All morning, they walk, they stop to rest, then they walk again. Izzy seems appreciative of everything. "Look at the trees," he says. "Look at those yellow leaves. Look at the sky, how blue."

By mid-morning, he's tired. He walks slowly, breathes with difficulty. Several times, Rachel asks him if he wants to go back home.

"No," he says, and he sniffs the air. "Somebody's burning leaves. The best smell."

They eat lunch in the same little place, where he has the maple-walnut ice cream again. Izzy picks at the walnuts, again barely eats anything. But he praises it. "Fine ice cream." And he praises the service and the restaurant. "Very nice atmosphere."

"I told you we'd come back." She's talking and smiling, but what she's really doing is watching him. Today, she's watching him every moment. Today, there's something about him that seems different. It's odd, but he's like someone very young: the bones in his face, in his cheeks and forehead, are shining; he criticizes nothing, everything is good.

They go out and walk again. Then they sit on a bench, watch people on the street. Rachel buys a bag of jelly beans, sorts out the licorice ones for Izzy. He eats two and gives her back the rest. "I'm having a good time," he says.

And again they walk, always staying on the sunny side of the street. Izzy lifts his face. "I always liked the sun."

They're on Baker Street when he stops in the middle of the sidewalk. Suddenly his face is covered with sweat. "I can't," he says. Just that. "I can't." He sways, can barely get out the words.

Rachel holds on to him, holds him with both arms. "Grandpa, don't fall down. Don't!" She looks around, sees a hardware store across the street. Somehow, clutching him, holding on to him, supporting him, she gets him there, gets him inside.

The woman behind the counter hurries, brings a chair. Izzy sits down. "Thank you ... just ... have to rest. ..." His voice is a whisper.

Rachel calls home. In ten minutes, Manny and Shirley are there. Large and reassuring, they rush into the store. Manny helps Izzy up, supports him toward the door. Shirley thanks the woman, thanks her over and over again. In the car, she sits directly behind her father, her arms around him.

Izzy seems to feel better. He sits in the passenger seat next to Manny and talks in his breathy voice. "Beautiful ... day. My granddaughter gave ... me a beautiful ... day."

Manny parks in the lot of the Loren Towers and they all go in. On Izzy's floor, just before they reach the door, he falls down. It happens quietly. One moment he is walking between them, the next he is on the floor.

* * *

184

"Ma, it's still the answering machine." Rachel has just dialed Dr. North's number for the third or fourth time.

Shirley leaves her post by the couch, where Izzy is lying, and takes the phone from Rachel. "Dr. North, this is Mrs. Cooper again. Dr. North I'm calling about my father, Mr. Shapiro. I called you once before. Please call me right back."

"If he doesn't call soon, we're taking Dad to the hospital," Manny says. "To the emergency room."

Shirley nods, sits down by the couch again.

Rachel pads around the apartment in her stocking feet. She can't sit still. She goes into the kitchen, looks in the refrigerator. Her stomach is gnawing shamelessly. In the cupboard she finds an ancient can of baked beans and dumps them into a pan. When they're heated, she brings the pan and three dishes into the living room. "Anybody hungry? I've got beans."

"I'll have a little," her father says. Her mother shakes her head. Rachel and her father sit down and eat the baked beans. The room is quiet, no sounds but Izzy's loud breathing and the clock in the kitchen with its crazy ticking. "This is good," her father says. And then, "I'm glad you were with him, sweetheart."

"I shouldn't have walked him all over the place."

"You said he wanted to stay out."

"Yes, but—" she shakes her head.

"Don't blame yourself. You can't dictate to Izzy. It's the disease. It could have happened in the middle of the night, when he was alone."

The phone rings. "I'll get it," Shirley says. It's Dr. North. "Yes. . . . Yes. . . . Yes, we'll meet you there." She gets off the phone. "Let's get Daddy ready. We're going to St. Joe's." She bends over Izzy.

185

"Daddy. Daddy, wake up." She moves his shoulder gently. "Daddy."

Rachel has never seen her grandfather so weak. With Manny's help, he goes to the bathroom. He takes a glass of water from Shirley and has to rest after drinking it. His voice is thready, fading away. To Rachel, he says, "Get me . . . a clean . . . shirt." To Shirley, he says, "My . . . shoes are . . . untied." And to Manny, "A lot of . . . bother." To each of them, one sentence, parceled out, and that's it, that's all he has the energy for.

The hospital is an old red brick building with narrow, high windows. Manny parks near the emergency entrance, and Rachel runs into the building to get a wheelchair for her grandfather. By the time she gets someone's attention, Izzy is inside, walking slowly between her parents. The nurse clicks her tongue. "You should have waited for me, sir."

Then Dr. North is hurrying toward them, hatless, his coat flying open. "Mr. Shapiro. What's this I hear? You've been overdoing things?"

"Me and the granddaughter . . . did a little . . . walking."

"Yes. Well, let's get you admitted and get some tests going. We'll see what's what here." The doctor squeezes Izzy's shoulder. His voice is calm, reassuring. "We'll get these tests run and probably have you out of here in a few days."

They move in a slow group toward the admitting office. The doctor hangs back with Manny. And Rachel, who's only a few steps ahead of them, hears the doctor say, "I don't think he'll be coming out again, Mr. Cooper."

THIRTY-FOUR

Rachel walks up and down the hospital corridor, one of an unending procession of patients, nurses, doctors, and visitors. Her parents are standing outside Izzy's room, leaning wearily against the lime-green walls. Fat Manny, tall Shirley. Rachel sees them through a blur: they look to her, suddenly, like characters in a cartoon, like people she might see on a street and pity. They've all been here for hours now.

Dr. North is in Izzy's room, tapping into his chest, drawing out the fluid in his lungs with a long needle. Rachel hears her grandfather's groans. She rushes away. She is light-headed, her stomach feels at once full and gnawingly empty. She takes in deep breaths, one after the other. The hall is narrow and the smell of the hospital—a mixture of things acrid, rotting, and cooking—clings to the walls.

She never should have agreed to Izzy's going out today. This wouldn't have happened. He needed to rest, not to walk and overdo things and exhaust himself. Why didn't she protest? Why didn't she throw her weight around a little, say, "No, Grandpa, I don't feel like it, I don't want to go out today, we're staying in." Ever since his collapse, she has been terrorized by one idea: that his weakness, his falling, is her fault. Yet only an hour ago, Dr. North told them that the weakness was caused by an accumulation of fluid in the lungs.

When Dr. North comes out of Izzy's room, he takes Shirley by the elbow. "We had to tap in five times—the tumors were in the way. But we got a pint of fluid. I think your father will be more comfortable now. You can all go home. He should sleep all right tonight. I'll look in on him tomorrow."

"Thank you, Doctor," Shirley says. "Thank you. Can I go see him? Can I say good night to him?"

"Of course. But he's probably sleeping."

They tiptoe into Izzy's room. He is asleep, his head tossed back, nose sticking into the air, mouth open. A gray film of beard shadows his cheeks.

"Where is he?" Shirley gasps the next morning. Rachel and her parents have just arrived at the hospital. Izzy is not in the room. The bed is empty; the closet door hangs ominously open.

"My God," Manny says.

A picture forms in Rachel's mind: two white-coated orderlies wheeling Izzy on a cart out of his room in the middle of the night. She runs into the hall. From another room, behind a closed door, she hears the sounds of a man laughing—no, sobbing. Izzy? She stands outside the room, then starts toward the nurses' station.

Then a door across the hall opens and Izzy emerges. He is wearing white-paper hospital slippers, holding a glass vial of urine in one hand and the back of the hospital gown in the other.

"Grandpa!"

"You're here?" he says calmly.

"Grandpa, how are you feeling?"

"How should I feel? They don't let you sleep in this place."

He's a marvel, he sounds like himself, he sounds grand to Rachel's ears. She follows him into the room. "Ma! Look who I found."

"You're here, too?" Izzy says to Manny. "What is this, a convention?" He allows Shirley to kiss him, then shuffles over to the chair near the window and sits down.

"Daddy, did you sleep all right?"

"Who sleeps? You're here to be made better. So the first thing is ... they tire you out so much, you take their treatment, no matter what."

They cluster around him. Rachel perches on the arm of his chair. "Grandpa, you've got an attitude problem."

"Listen ..." He looks at each of them in turn. "For my parents, going into the hospital ... was the worst thing that could happen. You went into the hospital for only one thing." He nods. "But today, it's different. Today, the doctors are much smarter."

THIRTY-FIVE

"I'm not going to school today, Ma."

"You don't feel good?" Shirley is standing at the counter drinking coffee. Her face is long and tense.

"I feel fine," Rachel says. "I want to go to the hospital and stay with Grandpa."

"You can go there right after school."

Rachel pushes aside her plate. "No. I want to go now. This morning."

"What, and spend the whole day in the hospital? You can't do that."

"Why not? When Daddy had that hernia operation last year, you spent the whole day in the hospital with him."

"That was different. You have to go to school, you can't just skip school for no good reason."

Rachel works hard to control her voice. "Ma, did you hear what you just said?"

"What? What did I say that was so terrible?"

"I didn't say terrible. I only asked you if you heard—no." She shakes her head, starts over again. "You said I can't skip school—if that's what you want to call it. I call it staying out. You said I can't stay out *for no good reason*. Grandpa's not a good reason?"

"Who said that?" Shirley's cheeks burn along the

bones. "That's not what I meant, Rachel. Don't twist my words around. I meant you're a schoolgirl. What you have to do is go to school. That's what you have to do."

"But not if I need to do something else that's more important."

"And who's judging that?"

"I am. I'm judging that."

Shirley puts down her cup, turns her back to Rachel. She sighs and sighs again.

Is she looking out the window? Is she thinking? Not thinking? Rachel can't tell. The only thing she can tell is that she wants, with an almost physical need, to be in the hospital with Izzy. She's heard that when she was a baby and wanted to go outside, she would rap her head against the window, and once rapped so hard that she cracked the glass. "Ma—" Her voice cracks. "Ma! Are you listening to me? You, of all people, you're the one who should understand."

Shirley turns around. She nods. "So go, Rachey, go if it means so much to you."

Izzy is sitting in the chair by the window when Rachel arrives. "Good morning, Grandpa."

He frowns. "What are you doing here?"

"What do you think? Checking up on you."

"Why aren't you in school?" He holds his cheek up for her to kiss.

"Because I'd rather be here. What'd you have for breakfast? Did you sleep okay?"

"Number-one question—they gave me pancakes. Too heavy. Number-two question—not bad. Any more? Get out your clipboard, write it down. That's what they all do."

Just then, a nurse wheels in a metal trolley with an intravenous bottle hooked up to it. She finds a vein in the back of Izzy's hand and punches into it. "I'm Tammy."

"I'm Izzy."

"Glad to meet you." She adjusts the rate at which the IV solution drips. "There we go." She makes a notation on the chart clipped to the end of the bed. "Now, if you want to take a walk, your little bottle of goodies has to walk with you, okay?"

"What's in the IV?" Rachel asks.

"Mostly potassium. . . . See you later, sweetheart," she says to Izzy.

Another nurse enters, wheeling in a green oxygen tank. "Hi," he says, "I'm Martin."

"Izzy Shapiro. Pleased to meet you."

"I'll be helping you out with oxygen, Mr. Shapiro. Having a little trouble breathing, are you, sir?" Martin speaks at the same loud pitch Tammy used. "This'll help. This will really make you feel more comfortable." He fits a clear, green plastic mask over Izzy's nose and mouth. A flexible, white plastic hose leads to the oxygen tank behind the bed.

Martin turns the valves, checks the meter. He writes on his clipboard. "You can take this oxygen mask off anytime you want to, Mr. Shapiro, but I think you'll feel better with it on."

Izzy nods. "Okay. Thank you."

A doctor in a long, starched white jacket enters. Her hair is in one thick braid down her back. A stethoscope hangs from her jacket pocket. She sits down on the bed next to Izzy. "I'm Dr. Greenbaum, Mr. Shapiro. I have a few questions for you." She has a clipboard in her lap.

"You're Jewish?" Izzy says.

Dr. Greenbaum looks surprised. "Yes."

192

Rachel's embarrassed. "Grandpa," she says, "why do you ask that?"

"I want to know some information. Is it so terrible? She's Jewish. That's nice to know." From behind the oxygen mask, his voice emerges, thin, muffled.

Dr. Greenbaum takes a medical history. "Is there a history of diabetes in your family? . . . Did anyone in your family have heart problems? . . . Cancer? . . . What kind? . . . What did your father die of? . . . How old was he? . . . Did your mother outlive him? . . . How many brothers and sisters? . . . When did they die?"

To Rachel's surprise, Izzy seems to enjoy answering the doctor's questions. "I had one brother and three sisters. Samuel, Anna, Bertha, and Martha. Do you want their birthdates, also?"

The doctor takes down the information. "Let me see, what did I miss? Oh, yes, here's one—did you ever have liver trouble in the past, Mr. Shapiro?"

Izzy pulls down the oxygen mask. "Are you inferring that I have liver trouble in the present?"

Dr. Greenbaum's eyebrows go up. "I see that I have to be precise with you."

When Dr. Greenbaum leaves, Izzy says, "She's a very nice girl."

"Grandpa, she's not exactly a girl."

"If she's not a girl, what is she? She didn't look like a man to me."

"She's a woman, Grandpa."

"That's what I said, Rachel. A very nice girl."

"Grandpa—*woman.*"

He waves his hand irritably. "Oh. That stuff. Don't start with me."

Rachel walks out of the room. "Going to the bathroom," she says as she leaves. In the bathroom, she washes, makes a face at herself in the mirror Why argue with Izzy now? "Use your head, Cooper."

When she goes back into the room, he's lying on his back, his hands folded over his stomach. "There you are," he says.

"Call of nature."

"Mmm-huh."

"Is the mask comfortable?"

"What?"

"Is the oxygen mask comfortable, Grandpa?"

"I can breathe better."

All day, doctors and nurses are in and out of the room, asking questions, listening to Izzy's heart, taking blood samples, checking his temperature and his blood pressure. Everybody writes everything down. "Did you evacuate today, Mr. Shapiro?" A nurse stands ready to write down his answer.

"Yesterday. Just my house."

"Well, you haven't lost your sense of humor."

Rachel watches, fascinated, as the nurse makes a note on her clipboard. Is she writing that down? Patient retains sense of humor.

Rachel's mother comes in the afternoon, having left work early. Her father shows up an hour or so later. Shirley has brought flowers, a bag of sesame rolls, and a waxed-paper-wrapped dill pickle. Manny comes with the newspaper and a chocolate bar.

"What for?" Izzy says with each gift. "Put it on the table. Put it right there."

They stay through his supper hour, eating their supper in the hospital cafeteria. "Go," Izzy says when they return. "Go. Don't stay so long." Every time he says it, they stay a little longer.

There's an old Marx Brothers comedy on TV.

"I've got to see this," Manny says, so they all watch it together.

Harpo toots his horn, rolls his eyes. Izzy takes down his oxygen mask to say, "That guy, he was something." And he makes a Harpo face.

They're all laughing when a nurse pokes in her head. "You people having a party in here?"

The next day, Rachel goes to the hospital again. She can't see any difference between skipping one day and skipping two days. "But this is the last time," her mother says. Rachel doesn't think so, but she doesn't argue. Not now.

She remembers to call Alice Farnum that day. "Hi, it's Rachel. Rachel Cooper."

"Hi, dear! Well, it's been a while."

"I know. I just—a lot of things have happened." She gives up trying to lead up to it gradually and tells Alice about Izzy bluntly, briefly.

"I'll come visit him," Alice says at the end of the call.

At her parents' insistence, Rachel goes back to school on Wednesday. As far as they are concerned, she is back in school where she belongs. As far as she is concerned, she belongs in the hospital and she's only here for the day. In every class, she stays behind for a few minutes, explains the situation with Izzy to each teacher, collecting her assignments for the week behind her and asking for the work for the following week. Most of her teachers are sympathetic; a few of them are annoyed but give her the work. Which is all she cares about.

She eats lunch with Helena, tells her what she's going to do. A frown crosses Helena's big, round, smooth face. "What's your mother going to say?"

"The same thing my father's going to say. No, you can't. You belong in school. Et cetera."

"And?"

"And?" Rachel shrugs, sighs. "I don't know, Helena. They're just going to have to accept it. I can't go to school with Izzy in the hospital. That's all I know right now."

After school, she meets Lewis and talks to him about her plans. They stand by the building and hug. Rachel puts her head against his chest. It seems so good to do that, just to let herself hug and think of nothing.

In the morning, she tells her parents she's going to the hospital. "You are not," Shirley says.

Rachel takes a deep breath. "Why do you say that?"

"You know why."

"Tell me again."

Both parents do, in detail: School for her is like work for them. She has a responsibility to go to school. This is what she does in the world, school is where she belongs. She can go to the hospital every day if she wants to, that's fine. But every day *after* school.

"Rachey, we don't know how long this is going to go on," her father says. He is trying sweet reason. "The doctor is not giving us numbers. Now, what if it's a month? Two months? Are you going to stay out of school two months?"

Shirley's approach is simpler. She's just stubborn. "I don't want you missing school. Period. End of discussion."

But it isn't, because Rachel is just as stubborn. She refuses to give up. She won't and she can't. It's not a matter now of should she go to the hospital, or can she or will she. She's going there. She wants to be with Izzy. The whole idea of how long it will go on is exactly the point.

How long will it go on? What if it's only a week? Or five days? What if two days are all he's got left and she's not there with him? No, with or without her parents' permission, she's going to do this thing.

She opens her notebook. "Here are all my assignments. I'm going to keep up with my work. You know I don't have any trouble keeping up. Remember when I was sick? It didn't make any difference. I'll do my homework, I won't fall behind. I promise you. Please," she says finally. "Please, just say yes."

THIRTY-SIX

Every morning, Rachel is in the hospital by eight-thirty. She wakes early these days. Her room is dim, and a gray light slips under the window shade. She turns over but cannot find the place to enter sleep again. She gets up, dresses, packs her knapsack with fruit, sandwiches, books, a hairbrush, and her journal.

She leaves the house, takes a bus to the hospital. She knows the quickest way to Izzy's room. Louise, a big, cheerful nurse, calls out, like Johnny Carson, "Heeeere's Rachel!"

When she walks into Izzy's room, he says, with a mixture of disapproval (he doesn't think she ought to be skipping school, either) and relief, "You're here again."

"Bad penny, Grandpa." She kisses him, refills his water glass, opens the curtains, finds a music station on the little portable radio that Manny bought for him. That's the start of her day in the hospital.

Izzy's day started hours ago. It's not a calm and quiet thing to be a sick person. He's already been down to X ray this morning. He's already tired out. He lies on the bed, his eyes fluttering. His hands look white, clean, bony. His breath is fast and shallow. He sits up, struggles to spit phlegm, struggles for each breath.

All morning, he sleeps and wakes, sleeps and

wakes. And each time he wakes, he checks the oxygen mask, his fingers playing over the plastic to make sure it's in place. When he takes it off to sip water, his skin tightens with fear and he quickly pushes it back on.

Around eleven o'clock, Martin comes in to give Izzy a breathing treatment. "Uh, Rachel, could you just step out?"

What's so private about breathing treatments? She doesn't say it. She waits meekly in the hall. She's not in charge. Izzy's not in charge, either. It's his life, his body, but he has almost nothing to say about it anymore. He has changed. His gruff command of his world is gone. Now he waits with the eager, anxious eyes of a boy for the words of nurses and doctors.

Standing in the hall, waiting for Martin to finish, Rachel remembers the way Izzy came into the hospital—weak but on his feet, a man living with an illness. Now he's become a patient. And a patient is unlike anyone else. Maybe it's like the difference between Army life and civilian life, only more so. There is no place in the life of a soldier for free will. Nor is there in the life of a patient.

The hospital staff are the supreme commanders. Izzy wakes at their prodding, he eats their food at their times, he takes their pills, submits to their tests and questions, sits up and lies down at their suggestions. Of course, there are no sergeants as in the Army, and really everyone is very kind. But it's the kindness of the healthy and the young for the old and the sick. They speak to him in loud, carrying voices, as if age and illness have affected not just heart and lungs, but also ears. In some ways this is what Rachel finds hardest to bear, to hear Izzy spoken to as if he's a deficient child.

199

No, what's hardest to bear is that he allows it to happen. She wants him to bark back, to say something sharp and edgy, to let the commanders of the Sick Corps know that he's more than a humble foot soldier who willingly and eagerly takes their orders. What she wants, really, is for him to be the way he's always been.

Dr. Greenbaum comes in. "Good morning, Mr. Shapiro."

"Doctor, how am I doing?"

"You're doing fine, Mr. Shapiro. We've got a little procedure here to do. Okay?" She smiles at him, turns to Rachel. "Would you mind leaving us for a couple of minutes?"

Rachel wants to know what the little procedure is. Dr. Greenbaum is brisk. "If I tell you now, I'm just going to have to tell your parents again later. So why don't we let me explain when they come." She pulls the curtain around Izzy's bed.

In the hall, Rachel walks up and down. She hears "Hello, dear" at one door. Groans at another. She walks quickly, burning off energy but not enough. She runs down the four flights of stairs into the lobby, buys a pack of gum in the gift shop, runs back up the stairs.

As soon as her parents show up, Izzy tells them, "Dr. Greenbaum, that little one who looks like she should still be in school, says I'm doing fine. I suppose she knows what she's talking about."

"Why, Dad, the smaller they come, the smarter they are," Manny says, and they all laugh and look at Rachel.

Later, when Izzy's supper is delivered, Shirley says, "Now look at this! Stringy turkey, canned peas, and instant mashed potatoes. This is not a food service. This is a garbage patrol." And again, they all

200

burst out laughing. In the hospital, Rachel notices, things strike you funny that wouldn't in the outside world.

But maybe, she thinks the next day when Dr. North shows up, that's because there's so much that doesn't strike you funny, so many things you don't want to hear, so much that's unpleasant and difficult and false.

Dr. North sits on the edge of Izzy's bed, asks a few questions, reads the chart, chats to Izzy about a basketball game he saw the night before.

"When can I go home, Doctor?"

Rachel looks out the window. Why does her grandfather ask this? Why is his voice light, hopeful?

"We have to stabilize your breathing, Mr. Shapiro." He takes out his stethoscope, listens to Izzy's chest.

"And when will that be?"

Dr. North rubs Izzy's arm. "Oh, I'm sure it won't be long."

Later, at supper, a nurse says to Izzy, "Honey, you didn't eat much. You have to eat to keep up your strength. Can you think of something else you'd like?"

Izzy turns his head away. His voice is low. "Nothing. Thank you. I have no hunger, I have no desire. Nothing."

THIRTY-SEVEN

"Hi, Rachel."

"Lewis? Hi!"

"Is this an okay time to talk?"

"Yes, it's great. We just got back from the hospital. Hold it a minute, Lewis. . . . Ma, don't worry, I'll get enough sleep. . . . Ma, please!"

"Rachel? Rachel, want me to call another time?"

"No, Lewis, hang on. I want to talk to you. . . . Ma, I'll be up pretty soon. . . . Lewis? Hi, I'm here again."

"Rachel, how's it going? I miss you in school. Today, especially. I wanted to go to Poppie's with you."

"I know. I thought about it, too."

"Did you go to work?"

"No, I'm not working anymore for a while."

"How come? Did you quit?"

"I told Martin, my boss, about Grandpa and got—I guess you'd call it a leave of absence."

"Did big Martin say 'I care'?"

"Very good, Lewis. I think he did. He was really nice about it. He said fine, just let him know when. . . . So what about you? What are you doing with yourself these days?"

"Thinking a lot about you."

"That's nice. Really?"

"True. How about you?"

"Lewis. I think about you. I do. But—"

"Yeah?"

"Don't be hurt. It's just that mostly what I think about is Grandpa and the hospital. I can't help it. Last night, I dreamed about it. This dream—it was so real. The nurses were changing Grandpa's bed, you know how they do—one on each side of the bed? And they each grab a piece of sheet? It all happened in the dream, each step. They hauled Grandpa up as if he weighed two ounces. And I thought, Oh, God, he's getting smaller and smaller, he's disappearing. And I woke up, and I felt so—I'm sorry. I didn't mean to be depressing."

"No, I'm glad you're, you know, telling me what you feel."

"Lewis, if I told you everything I feel—I couldn't. I don't even know what I feel sometimes. There's so much, I almost feel numb . . . Wait. Wait. Let's change the subject. Do you hate people who tell you their dreams? My mother's always telling my father her dreams, and every time she does it, I think I am *never* going to tell anyone my dreams. And I just did it."

"Better me than some other poor victim. Oh, I should tell you. Exciting day in Alliance High. Fire drill."

"Did Vandermeer get out there with his megaphone and tell everyone what a rotten drill they carried out?"

" 'People of Alliance High, you do not take this fire drill *seriously* enough.' "

" '*If* there was a real fire emergency, *which* we are very fortunate there was *not*—' "

" '—you would not be standing around here *laughing and talking* while I am trying to get across to you the *essential gravity* of this *occurrence!*' I bet that gives you a nostalgic pang for old Alliance High."

"This morning, I almost went to school."

"Why didn't you? Afraid you'd never be able to tear yourself away again?"

"I woke up and I thought, Why not go to school today, just check in? I planned what I'd wear, my black skirt, my long-sleeved yellow blouse—you're not interested in these details, are you?"

"Rachel, carry on. Black skirt, yellow blouse, I like that, I'm getting the picture. Would you braid your hair?"

"You like it in braids?"

"Remember that day in the library? You had this bunch of braids."

"I didn't know you remembered that. Okay, I'll braid my hair. I was going to wear a black tie, too."

"A tie?"

"Yeah, black tie on the yellow blouse. So I've got my clothes all picked out and I go downstairs and pack my lunch and I think about seeing you in school."

"Okay, I'm with you. And?"

"And, I don't know what, Lewis—just what I've been telling you, I guess. Twenty minutes later, I was on my way to the hospital."

"Okay, Rachel. Maybe I'll get to see you this weekend. What do you think?"

"I want to."

"Me, too."

"I've got to hang up now, Lewis."

"Okay. Bye, Rachel. I—you know, I really like you."

"Me, too, to you, Lewis."

"What? I can't hear you."

"I really like you, Lewis."

204

THIRTY-EIGHT

They all eat supper in the cafeteria. Rachel is hungry, eats a full plate of macaroni and cheese, but Shirley barely tastes her food. "I hate this hospital food. I hate it. And this is what they give Daddy. It's a crime."

The next day, Shirley brings a jar of homemade soup, unscrews the lid, and says, "Smell, Daddy. Isn't that a delicious smell?"

In his new, thin voice, Izzy whispers, "Take it away. They give me a special diet, Shirley. I have to eat the food they give me."

The food service cart rattles through the hall. The attendant brings in Izzy's meal, places it on the bed tray. Rachel winds up his bed so he can sit up. Shirley removes the metal cover from the plate, takes one look at the food, and exclaims, "Daddy, if you eat that cow patty instead of my good soup, I'm disowning you."

From under the oxygen mask comes Izzy's snorting laughter.

The next day, though, Izzy isn't laughing about anything. Overnight, he's shed his meek and hopeful attitude and become a furious man. He's angry with Rachel, angry with Shirley and Manny, angry with the doctors and the nurses. Sitting up to cough, he gasps and chokes. "I can't walk . . ." he whispers angrily, "I can't breathe ... I can't even spit up what's in my chest. What's left?"

He lies awake for hours, fighting sleep, staring at the ceiling. Rachel sits by the bed, makes a pretense of studying. Her eyes go continually to her grandfather. "Grandpa?" He doesn't answer. Where is he? What is he thinking? Is he in pain?

Once, under the mask, he mumbles her name. "What, Grandpa?" she says at once. "Do you want something? Can I get you something?"

He turns his face away. He won't talk to her. He won't talk to anyone. He stares at the ceiling.

The nurses give him pills for pain, take his temperature and his blood pressure, check the IV, talk to him coaxingly or sweetly or heartily. "How are you today, lovey? Come on now, aren't you going to say hello to me? And I thought you liked me.... Well, this isn't like you, Mr. S., I'm disappointed!"

He answers nothing, remains mute, stubborn, enclosed in himself and his anger. Only once, when a nurse asks if he wants his bed rolled down, he replies in a low, almost inaudible voice, "That's where I'm going—down, down, down."

Later, when Shirley comes, she bends over him, holds his hand, kisses him.

"Dad," Manny says, standing at the foot of the bed, "they tell me you didn't eat all day. You have to eat."

"What for?"

"You have to keep up your strength."

"What for?" Then he stops talking again. He won't say anything; nothing, not a word. But when they're ready to leave, he sits up suddenly, points to Shirley. "Ask the doctor when I can go home. I want to go home." And he takes off the oxygen mask, rips it off his nose, looks desperately around, as if he'll fling it away. He gasps for air, his head trembles, and as if for dear life, he holds on to the bars on either side of the bed.

Then, panting for breath, his mouth open for air, he falls back on the pillow and with trembling fingers puts the oxygen mask on again.

THIRTY-NINE

JOURNAL •

Sunday night — at home. All day today, Grandpa had a lot of pain. It's terrible to watch and be able to do nothing. Ma was beside herself; she couldn't take it and left, finally. "I feel helpless, helpless," she said. "I'll be back later."

She went out—and Alice Farnum walked in. And it was amazing what happened, amazing what Grandpa did. All that pain, and when Alice showed up, he made himself—what should I say? pleasant? happy? No, welcoming, that's it—he made himself welcoming for her. He talked to her, he smiled, he made a little joke.

And then, when she left, he lay back and everything seemed to go out of his face. He was exhausted. He gasped for air, he clawed the air for air. I thought he was dying. I thought it was happening. And I couldn't breathe either.

Monday—in the hospital. Today, Grandpa wouldn't eat his lunch. He lay back, one hand on each side of the bed, gripping the bed bars, looking into space.

"Grandpa, won't you eat a little bit? This applesauce looks good."

"No."

"I could get you something else. You want some sherbet? I'll go down to the cafeteria—"

"No."

"Can I get you anything?"

"No. No one can do anything for me."

He's dying. He really is dying. I keep saying it to myself so I can believe it.

No one says it. No one says, *Izzy Shapiro is dying*. Not me, not Ma, not Daddy, not the nurses, not the doctors. We don't say it to each other and we don't say it to him. We're like weather forecasters who only want to report sunshine.

Dr. North says, "Doing pretty good today, Mr. Shapiro."

Martin says, "Those breathing treatments help you, did they, sir?"

Daddy says, "When you get out of here, Dad, we'll have a party."

And Dr. Greenbaum says, "Let us know if you have any pain, Mr. Shapiro. No need to be uncomfortable."

Tuesday morning—in the hospital. Grandpa is sleeping. He sleeps a lot more now than he did even a few days ago. Sometimes he talks in his sleep, little odd words and phrases like "the red jar" or "teepees, too many teepees." When he's awake, though, he speaks carefully. I can understand everything he says, and everything he says makes sense.

My schoolwork is done. I have nothing to do but look at Grandpa sleeping—and think. Last night, Dr. North was here. As soon as he was done with Grandpa, Ma and Daddy and I got together with him in the hall outside Grandpa's room. That's our conference room. That's the place where the truth is told.

We huddled out there, as if we were planning tactics for a football game. Daddy said, "How is he, Dr. North?"

"Oh, not too bad."

"But he's having so much trouble breathing."

"Yes. The tumors."

Ma said, "Every day it's harder for him to breathe, Doctor. Every day."

"Because the tumors are growing. They're taking up more space in his lungs."

"The tumors?" Ma said. Dr. North nodded. Ma said it again. "The tumors?" And there was this quivery, hopeful sound in her voice, as if maybe Dr. North would say, "No, no, did I say tumors? I meant *humors.*"

Wednesday—home. Everyone's sleeping, except me. I come home from the hospital so tired I think I'm going to fall dead asleep, and then I lie here and think of things, think about Grandpa. So now I've turned on the light again to write here.

Tonight, we were all in Grandpa's room. It was around nine o'clock, almost time for us to leave. The room was dim. We were whispering, because we thought Grandpa was sleeping. He hadn't said anything for a long time, just groaned and turned and mumbled words. Then suddenly, he said very clearly, "What's the date?"

"Is he awake?" Ma whispered.

"I'm awake." For a moment he sounded exactly like he always did, just like himself. "What's the date?"

I went over to him. "It's November twelfth, Grandpa."

He turned his head back and forth. "Thanksgiving is soon. I won't make it."

Ma leaned over the bed. "Daddy, you will. We'll all be together for Thanksgiving."

"What's the weather?"

"Now?" Ma said. "Now it's dark outside, dark and chilly."

"The weather," he said. "Today. The *weather*."

I said, "It was pretty cold today, Grandpa."

"How cold?"

"Not cold enough for me to wear a scarf, but cold enough for Ma to say, 'Rachel, wear a scarf.' " I was trying to be amusing. I notice that we all do it, we keep making cute or funny remarks. It's for Grandpa's benefit, and if one of us scores, if we make him smile the least bit, we all get tremendously happy.

"The sky was blue?" His voice was urgent. "Was it sunny?"

"The sun was out all day," Daddy said. "I took my lunch and ate it in the park."

"It's fall," Grandpa said. "You had a beautiful fall day." He closed his eyes.

"Daddy?" Ma said. Then she put her finger to her lips and whispered, "Shhh, he's sleeping."

But I thought, No, he's gone away, left us. He doesn't want to be with people who can get up and walk out of the hospital, people who can eat lunch in the park and see the sun and the sky.

Thursday morning—in the hospital. Just a little while ago, Dr. North stopped in. "Mr. Shapiro, how are you?"

211

"You tell me. How am I, Doctor?" He panted to get the words out. I thought it couldn't be any harder for Grandpa to breathe, and now it's become harder still. "Any . . . better? I hurt. Why do I hurt?"

"The heart is working hard, Mr. Shapiro. I'll increase the number of shots you receive. That should help." He chatted up Grandpa for a moment, then he left.

Ate my lunch in the cafeteria. Looked at all the other people eating lunch, all "civilians" like me, and wondered who they were, who they were here for.

All afternoon Grandpa keeps falling asleep, then waking up. Every time he wakes up he asks, "What time is it?"

And I tell him.

Then he falls asleep again. But sometimes he can't fall asleep. He's in too much pain. He groans and talks in a low voice to himself. "No, Izzy," he says, "don't complain." Or sometimes he says, "Izzy, hold out."

The nurse just came in with Grandpa's shot. He whispered to her, "You got here. I tried to hold out. I'm trying not to complain."

Thursday night—home. Ma and Daddy are in the kitchen. I can hear their voices, Daddy's rumble, Ma's voice, higher and breaking. Tonight, when we were ready to leave the hospital, at the end of visiting hours, Grandpa was sleeping. We tiptoed around, getting our stuff.

Then Grandpa's eyes opened and he half sat up. "Oh, you're going," he said. His voice was clear. "Oh, it's a long time until midnight. It's a long time until morning."

Ma kissed him. "Daddy, darling, try to sleep."

He patted her face, nodded, and patted her face again. On the way home, Ma cried and cried.

Friday afternoon—in the hospital. This morning when I got here, Grandpa's bed was cranked up and he looked good, he had color in his face. He looked healthy. I got excited. I thought—I don't know what I thought. Did I really think he was getting better? When I saw Martin in the hall, I told him how good Grandpa looked.

"Oxygen flush, honey."

Saturday night—home. Today, all day, Grandpa went in and out of sleep and kept asking strange questions in a slurry voice. "Do the musicians play tins? Where's the red jeer? What about his onion hands?"

Louise said it might be from the drugs or it might be from lack of oxygen. She wrote it all down on his chart.

The worst moment came when we were ready to leave. Grandpa said, "You're leaving?"

"We'll be back in the morning," Ma said. "I'll bring you some fresh orange juice, the real thing."

Grandpa didn't answer. I thought he was sleeping. Then he said, "I can't sleep now. No. Can't sleep. Not now." He rolled his head on the pillow.

"You don't feel sleepy?" Ma said.

"Not that."

"What is it?"

"You know."

Ma leaned close to him. "No, tell me."

"Don't dare . . ."

213

"What? Don't dare what?"

"Sleep. Can't sleep at night."

"Why?"

"You know."

Ma looked around at me and Daddy. "He's afraid."

Daddy sat down next to Grandpa and took Grandpa's hand. "Dad," he said, "it's all right, you can close your eyes. It's all right. I'll stay here with you."

"Go home."

"No, I'm staying," Daddy said. "I'll sleep right here, I can sleep in this chair."

"Manny, no," Ma whispered. "You'll be a wreck in the morning."

"Tomorrow's Sunday," he whispered back. "I'll sleep all day. I don't have anything else to do." Daddy held Grandpa's hand. "Shirley and Rachel are going home, but I'm staying, Dad. I'm staying right here."

Grandpa closed his eyes. In a few minutes, he was asleep.

Sunday morning—in the hospital. Ma is sitting by Grandpa's bed, eating a sweet roll and leafing through a magazine. I've got the other chair by the window. As soon as we came, Daddy went straight home to shower and eat and sleep. He'll be back later. Grandpa's asleep again. Or is he awake? It's hard to tell. Awake or asleep, his hands move over the covers, he groans and chews on his tongue.

Later. When Grandpa coughs, which he does all the time, trying to get that stuff out of his lungs, he half sits up, he grabs the bars and he coughs with deep groans; he coughs huge, hoarse, loud, dry, retching, groaning coughs, and the blood vessels in his forehead swell and throb. Then he falls back on the bed, panting, and Ma wipes his face with a washcloth and I fill his water glass and put a new straw in it. For once, I think Ma and I feel the same thing—helpless.

Monday—in the hospital. All morning Grandpa has been restless. He moves from side to side, can't hold still, moves as if a thousand ants are crawling over his skin, moves and groans and whispers, "Oh, please, do something for me."

When I couldn't bear it another moment, I ran into the hall. I found the charge nurse and asked her if she would give Grandpa something for pain. She checked his chart. "No, it's not time yet for his medication."

"When will it be?"

"Not for another hour."

"But he's in pain."

"I'll speak to the doctor, see if he wants to increase the dosage."

"Thank you." I thought I'd done something until I went back into the room and saw Grandpa moving back and forth and heard him groaning.

Tuesday—in the hospital. Grandpa slept almost all morning. Just now, he woke up and called for Ma, then for Daddy. "Shirley. Manny."

I bent over the bed. "I'm here, Grandpa."

"Help me."

"What do you want, Grandpa?"

"Help me . . . sit up."

Yesterday, he could sit up alone.

I put my hand in the small of his back and

shoved him upright. He wanted to sit up so he could cough. He coughed and coughed, panted, gasped, coughed. "Oh, help," he said, choking and gasping. "Help me, help me." Then he lay down and fell asleep, as exhausted as if he'd run twenty miles.

Later. Ma's here. She told me Dr. North has ordered more breathing treatments for Grandpa, more codeine. She said, "Rachey, don't you think he's lost weight?"

Yes, he's lost weight. He's shrinking. He's smaller. He used to be such a big man. Now I have a little grandfather, a small man in a white hospital gown. His arms are all bones, his eyes stare out of his face.

FORTY

"Rache, come on," her mother says Tuesday night. She glances at the people crowding into the elevator past Manny. "*Rachel*. Stop dreaming."

Rachel's father is holding the elevator open for her, but she doesn't go in. She *cannot* go in. Something is holding her back. She is not dreaming, yet the sensation, vague but compelling, is something very like a dream. She cannot move, her feet are stuck, her knees as tight as if bound by wires.

"Rachel." Her father's voice sharpens against her slowness. "You're keeping other people waiting."

From the elevator people glance at her, then at her father. She sees their smiles, tolerant or annoyed. And even this is not enough to move her.

"Well, is she coming or isn't she?" someone says from the back.

She finds her voice. "Dad, go ahead."

"What?"

"I'm not going with you."

"Okay, she's not going," the same voice calls from the elevator. "Is it okay if the rest of us leave?"

Her parents glance at each other and step out. "What is it?" her mother says. "What's the matter?"

"I'm not going home with you." She hadn't known she was going to say that. But it's right. At

217

once, she hears a voice, like an order: *Don't leave him. Don't leave Izzy tonight.*

"Not going home?" her mother repeats. "What do you mean? You can't go home alone. The buses aren't running. It's too late."

"I'm going to stay here overnight." She doesn't try to explain. Not the voice. But she says, "I have a feeling that I should—"

"Feeling? What feeling? What are you talking about?"

"Never mind," her father says, "let's not get into the feeling things. Rachel, you can't stay overnight. You won't sleep. I know. Saturday, I didn't sleep all night."

"I don't care, Daddy. It's not that important."

"You need your sleep," her mother says.

"Ma, don't worry. Maybe I will be able to sleep on the chair. It will probably be easier for me than for Daddy."

Shirley doesn't seem to hear her. "What's the matter with you? I never heard such a thing. Other people go to school and sleep at home. Why do you have to be so different?" Her eyes redden with anger and grief. "What did I do that I have a daughter like this?"

Standing there, waiting for her to come to her senses, her parents are like two large, tired animals. Her father puts his arm heavily across Rachel's shoulders and moves her toward the elevator. "Enough of this. It's not fair to your mother, darling."

Fear spurts from Rachel's belly to her throat; now she will do what they want. It will be the way it was when she was six and told her parents that she couldn't go to school anymore. They petted her and

218

said, "Oh, oh, sure you want to go to school," and they kissed her and laughed at her and sent her off. "You'll be fine," they said, "there's nothing to be afraid of."

But she knew what she knew. She was afraid of Luke Fowler, who was ten and liked to knock down little girls and kiss them with big, wet, mean kisses. "Don't worry about a thing," her parents said, and she went to school and Luke Fowler knocked her down, and she knew she had been right and they had been wrong.

Rachel looks at her mother. Her coat is buttoned wrong, the hem hangs lopsided.

She looks past her mother, through the window, to the darkness outside, then farther, to the pale fringe of light rising from the city. How hard it is to do anything! Hard for her to do what she wants to do, what she needs to do, which is only to stay with her grandfather tonight.

"Come," her father says. He presses the elevator button. "We're going home."

But Rachel is not six anymore, and in a very soft voice, she says, "No, I'm not going home tonight." She must speak in this soft voice because otherwise she will yell.

"You *are* coming home," her mother says.

"*No,*" Rachel says. And now she and her mother are looking at each other across a plain, a vast open, dry distance. And her father's arm is still on her shoulders. She moves out from under him.

"Ma—"

"What?"

She moves closer to her mother and rebuttons her mother's coat. "Do you want to stay, too?"

"Me? With you?"

Rachel nods. "Yes, Ma. We'll both stay with Grandpa." For a moment, the air between them is clear and they see each other.

"Oh, should I?" her mother says.

"No, you can't," Manny says. "No, Shirl. You can't stay up all night. You need your rest."

And now it's finishing. Rachel rises on tiptoe, kisses her mother. "I'll be all right. I'll call you tomorrow morning." She walks away from them. In a moment, she hears the creak of the elevator door.

Izzy's breath is noisy in the room. Rachel puts her head back against the chair. The room is shadowy. Izzy's cheekbones jut up. His breath is gaspy, labored. She begins to breathe with him. In . . . out . . . in . . . out. . . . The room is breathing with him, the bed breathes, the chair, the walls, the air itself breathes with him.

Martin comes in to check the oxygen tank. "Staying the night?" He doesn't seem surprised.

Around midnight, Izzy wakes. His skin is hot. She wipes his face and neck with a damp cloth. "Water," he says. He sips through the bent straw. He goes back to sleep, but an hour later, he's awake again. Or is he? What he says, quite clearly, is, "No ticket."

"Grandpa?" Rachel bends toward him. "I'm here, Grandpa."

"Hold my hand." She takes his hand, holds it, caresses it, and he falls asleep. Moments later, he wakes up again. "Hold me, hold me back," he exclaims. "Hurry!" She moves closer, puts her arms around him. "Harder," he gasps. She holds him so tightly her arms ache. He falls asleep and she releases him.

She curls up in the chair with the blanket Martin

brought her thrown over her legs. She watches Izzy in the dim light, her eyes stinging and burning. Finally, she can no longer keep her eyes open and falls asleep. When she wakes up hours later, it's not dark, but it's not yet light.

She pushes aside the blanket, stands up stiffly. Her mouth is dry, her legs ache from her cramped sleeping position. She does a few stretches, rolls her shoulders, and looks in her knapsack for her hairbrush.

"I don't have my ticket," Izzy says. She turns. He is sleeping. His voice is low but clear. "Can I see the captain?" Then, a moment later, "Take another boat!"

Rachel goes to him. Sweat bursts out on his face. She wets a cloth, wipes his cheeks and forehead. He's cold, icy cold—his forehead, his cheeks, his hands and arms, all cold. She wants to warm him and starts tucking the blankets around him.

His eyes open. "Hold my arms," he cries. "Hold my face. Is that you?"

"I'm here, Grandpa. I'm here." As she holds him, he becomes colder and colder; icy sweat pours off him. She grabs a wad of tissues and wipes his forehead. The tissues come away soaked. Suddenly, his head droops to one side, there's a rattling noise in his throat. She jumps back, frightened. He coughs twice, his head jerks, and there's another rattle deep in his throat.

"Grandpa?" His mouth is open. His nose juts into the air. "Grandpa? Grandpa!" A cry bursts out of her and she runs into the corridor.

A nurse walks toward her. "My grandfather," Rachel says. "My grandfather." Her eyes are throbbing. The nurse turns sharply into Izzy's room and

Rachel follows her. The nurse takes Izzy's pulse and blood pressure, shines a flashlight into his eyes. "I'll get the doctor."

Rachel stands at the foot of the bed. Why can't she breathe? Izzy's head is toppled to one side. He has a birdlike look, and she doesn't recognize the face.

A fat, young doctor with walrus whiskers comes in. In a little voice, he asks her to please step out. "Just for a minute, please." In the corridor, she leans against the wall.

The doctor comes out of the room. "I'm sorry. . . . You're the . . ."

"Granddaughter."

"He's dead."

"Yes." She knew that when she called the nurse. Then she understands. Her grandfather isn't officially dead until a doctor says so.

"Are you all right?" the doctor says.

She finds a tissue, blows her nose. "Yes."

"You were with him?"

"Yes."

"You've been staying nights?"

"No. Just tonight I wanted to."

"I see." He stares at her. "Well, is there someone you ought to call?"

She nods. She walks down the hall to the phone and calls home. Her father answers on the second or third ring. His voice sounds groggy with sleep. "Daddy, it's Rachel. Grandpa's dead. He just died."

"Wait a minute. What'd you say, sweetheart? Are you all right?"

She has to repeat it. "Grandpa's dead."

"We'll be right there. Are you all right?"

When she goes back to the room, two more nurses are coming out. "Are you all right, honey?" Why is everyone asking her that? She's alive. She's healthy. She's here.

She goes into the room. In these few minutes, something has changed. Izzy is in the same position, still lying flat on his back, but he looks different: he looks alive again. She goes closer, touches him. The warmth has returned to his skin. How did that happen? His skin feels normal, warm and elastic. The sunken, starved look is gone, too—he looks gaunt but better than he has for days and days. Too bad she can't tell Izzy, he might like this joke: Grandpa, you look better dead than you did alive.

Then her parents are there. Manny is crying. It's Shirley who puts her arm around Rachel. "Come away, Rachey, come away, it's too hard."

But even now, Rachel doesn't want to go. She holds the rails of the bed and she thinks, *I won't see him again. I want to see him again and I won't. I'll never see him again.*

FORTY-ONE

On a sheet of paper found, oddly enough, in the medicine cabinet in his apartment, Izzy had left instructions in his rather stiff, ornate handwriting about his death. The paper is discovered by Manny the day after Izzy's death, folded and taped to the inside of the cabinet door with the notation "To my family." And it says, simply, "I don't want a funeral. I don't want to be buried. Cremation. No fuss. No speeches. These are my requests. I'm in sound mind and I know what I want. Isadore Shapiro." The date under his signature was several weeks before he entered the hospital.

"I keep remembering how he asked the doctor, 'When can I go home?' " Shirley says. Her voice breaks. "I never knew for sure if he wanted to go home because he knew he was dying, or if he just wanted to go home, get out of the hospital."

"He knew, Ma," Rachel says from the chair where she's curled up, but there's so much noise in the living room, no one hears her. Everyone seems to be carrying on at least two conversations, talking about Izzy and catching up on news. The radio is on, a classical station, something somber, full of drumbeats. And Rachel's brother Phil, who's taken up bird-watching over the past year, is showing his father a wild bird caller, twisting the little red gadget to bring forth a gurgle of high-pitched bird sounds.

"Now I think he wanted to die at home and he didn't. He couldn't. I couldn't take him home, could I?" Shirley looks around the room for confirmation.

Manny gives the wild bird caller a twist. Birds twitter in the air. "You couldn't, Shirl."

"Maybe he still thought he really would get to go home, Grandmother," MB says. She and Phil had flown in the night before from Spokane. "Don't be sad." Sitting on the arm of the couch, she pets Shirley's hair. "I'm so glad to see you, Grandmother." Shirley looks up with a soft, grateful, and adoring gaze and leans her head against MB.

Rachel remembers how her mother had hugged MB in the airport, kissed her and hugged her and kissed her again and again, seeming to draw some comfort from her that she couldn't draw from Rachel. She had watched this with a hot beating of her heart, and then, like pulling a splinter just below the surface of the skin, leaving it sore but not painful, she had understood. Her mother is to MB as Izzy was, finally, to her, Rachel. Her mother is MB's grandparent, as Izzy was her grandparent, and a whole world of feeling is in that word.

For years she and Izzy, for whatever reasons, had been locked out of that world of feeling. It was only his illness, his dying, that had opened it to them, and though he never gazed at her in that totally accepting way that Shirley looks at MB, though he never leaned his head against her in quiet adoration, he had wrapped his arm across her shoulder protectively when the white dog menaced her, he had talked to her, he had depended on her, and he had said to her, "Go home, darling." He had called her "darling." He had spoken to her that way. *Go home, darling.*

A shudder, a shiver, a coldness, then a sensation

225

of warmth passes through Rachel. Memories of her grandfather rise up in her mind. "Aha, aha, aha!" as he won the game of Scrabble. Breaking eggs into a bowl: "The secret is in adding a bit of water. . . ." Bending over the stone wall: "You see this stone-work, straight as the day it was done. . . ." And then, other images and words, gleaming like bits of col-ored glass underwater: "The truth, just tell me the truth, do they have a name for this disease? . . . I went in swimming every day, hoping to meet her. . . . Licorice, I like anything licorice. . . ."

That night, Rachel and MB stay up late talking. "I'm really sorry to lose my great-grandfather," MB says, leaning on her elbow, "but I hardly knew him. It was always, once a year, just me and Daddy and Grandmother going over for a visit in the after-noon."

"Anyway, he wasn't easy to know," Rachel says. "Even if you lived here, not all the way across the country—"

"Yeah. He seemed so different from Daddy and Grandfather. . . . You were kind of quiet today. But calm. I don't think you're always that quiet. I guess you were closer to him."

Rachel nods.

"That's neat. I really love Grandfather, too. He's sweet, you know?"

"Uh-huh."

"Grandmother said Great-Grandfather was sick just for a couple of months. My other grandmother, my mom's mom, was incredibly sick for a whole year with some kind of kidney thing. Then she got better. Two months doesn't seem very long for someone as old as Great-Grandfather to be sick be-fore they die."

"It was long enough," Rachel says, and maybe she's a little sharp, because MB leans across the space between their two beds and says, "Hey, Rachel, hey, Auntie, I'm sorry, I didn't mean anything by it."

"That's okay." Rachel pulls up the covers and then, hearing herself breathe, remembering Izzy's struggles to breathe and their walks and his last days in the hospital, she thinks, No, it's true, it wasn't very long, not very long to have with someone. No time, really, no time at all, but it was all the time we had.

In the morning, before she does anything else, even before she dresses, Rachel calls Alice Farnum. "My grandfather died two days ago, Alice."

"Oh, Rachel." Alice starts crying.

Her tears, like little bullets, shatter Rachel's fragile calm. She feels a fierce and sudden push of resentment at Alice's easy sympathy, her quick sorrow. *Don't you dare cry, Alice. You hardly knew him.*

"Rachel, come see me, won't you? Let's not lose touch."

"Yes."

"Rachel? I mean it. I'll call you."

"Alice . . ." Her voice suddenly wobbles. "Thank you. I'll call you, too."

She goes into her room, closes the door. MB is still sleeping, still on Pacific time. Rachel stares at herself in the mirror. *Don't you dare cry. . . .* To even think of saying a thing like that to Alice . . .

She gathers up her clothes, walks down the hall to the bathroom. In the shower, she shampoos her hair, driving her hands hard into her scalp. "At least I only thought it, I didn't say it," she tells herself. She stands in the shower with her face raised, receiving

227

cold water, half a blessing, half a punishment. In the days since Izzy died, she has been like this, balancing between extremes, tears at one moment, absolute calm at the next. She is like someone crossing a rushing stream, precariously balancing on a log thrown across the treacherous waters.

After breakfast, she and her mother drive to the airport to pick up Jeremy. Seeing him come down the stairs and push through the glass door, Rachel's first impression is that he's exactly the same as when she last saw him—the beard, the dark eyes, the quick, jaunty walk—and that he's even wearing the same faded jeans and the same black T-shirt. Then, as he gets closer, she sees that he's put on a little weight, that there are faint, fine lines like the marks of tiny seashells beneath his eyes.

"Rachel. Mom. Hey, hey, hey, double-barreled welcome." He puts out his arms, hugs them both at the same time. "You guys look great." Only a sudden, deep flush of blood into his cheeks shows his emotion.

On the way home, he sits in the front seat next to Shirley, glancing back at Rachel now and then with a smile. Shirley, who usually drives sedately and well, sends the car hurtling forward, then slows down so much, a car in back of her gives her a loud, jeering horn. "I shouldn't be driving, I'm too excited," she says, looking at Jeremy, then back to the road. "I can hardly believe you're here, sweetheart. And our family is all together again. For the first time in I don't know how long. Because of Grandpa."

"Yeah," Jeremy says, "it's ironic, isn't it?" He turns around to Rachel.

His smile is an invitation to talk, and Rachel wants to respond, wants to say something about

Izzy, something real about his death, maybe about the dizzying amount of sheer busy-ness that has followed it. As her mother chops up the miles, still racing and then slowing on the drive home, Rachel wills herself to say something, but the memory of all the letters she's written Jeremy, all the feelings she's poured out in their raw state to this brother she hardly knows, keeps her shy and silent. She barely speaks, either then or later. Just looks at Jeremy—looks and wonders.

At lunch, the voices around the table rise and fall, food is passed, and Rachel, looking around, counts everyone off in her mind. Ma, Daddy, Phil, MB, Jeremy. Adds herself—Rachel. Thinks, *My family.* And for the first moment since her grandfather's death, feels happiness. Even though she grew up without her brothers and so, presumably, couldn't miss what she didn't know, hasn't she always missed having them here? Felt a gap in her life? In the same way in which, without knowing him, she missed being a part of her grandfather's life?

"If your mother and brother were here," Shirley is saying to MB, repeating the comment she made in the car, "our whole family would be together. It's almost the whole family, anyway, all together for the first time in years. And I think that's wonderful."

"And I say, let's all thank Grandpa," Jeremy says.

Shirley blushes. "No, no, no. No, I didn't mean that." And suddenly she starts to cry.

"Dammit, lay off her," Phil says to his brother.

"Man, what did I do?" Jeremy puts his arm around Shirley. "Sorry, Ma. I didn't mean—"

"It's all right, it's all right." She pats his arm. "I'm weepy." She wipes her eyes on her napkin. "Go on, everybody, go on eating. I'm fine."

But still, for a moment, things look bad. Jeremy fingers his beard, looking slit-eyed at Phil. And Phil, buttering and folding a slice of bread in half, returns a calm, disapproving glance. "What's the matter, Brother?" he says.

Then Manny steps in. "You two boys—please!"

"Boys!" MB exclaims. *Boys!* And the tension breaks, everyone laughs, and Jeremy playfully slaps Phil's outstretched hand.

But Rachel leaves the table. As suddenly as counting out her family at the table had made her happy, the sudden flare-up of tempers has made her unhappy. She's like a barometer responding to every hint of emotional weather. When her mother started crying, Rachel's eyes watered. When Phil gave Jeremy that steady, slow shake of the head, her heart speeded up, and when Jeremy's cheeks reddened, her own face burned with an answering emotion.

In the kitchen, she runs the cold water, fills a glass. Beyond her, in the dining room, she hears the voices of her father and MB. She sips the water slowly, almost luxuriously. It tastes so good. And then she thinks, Grandpa will never drink another glass of water. She leans on the counter, bends her head down into her hands. Grandpa will never lean against anything again. He will never . . . never . . . never . . . *anything* again.

Then, behind her closed eyes, she sees a road, a narrow, sandy road with large trees on both sides, and she sees herself walking down this road in the rain . . . dark, black-green of the trees . . . hard, dark lines of water sleeting down. . . .

For a moment, then, she is both in the kitchen and there, in the rain, on that narrow dirt road. And then she is only there and nothing else exists but the wet road, the trees lashed by wind, and herself, a solitary figure walking in the rain.

That afternoon, Rachel and Jeremy drive to the crematorium to pick up Izzy's ashes. She holds the plain, square box in her lap, trying to believe that this is all that's left of her grandfather. "It's heavy," she says.

"There're bits of bone in there, it's not just ashes."

"God."

"I know."

At home, no one knows where to put the box. "Should I put it on your desk, Daddy?" Rachel says.

Manny blanches. "No, I don't like that. I don't like the idea of Izzy in there, that that's all there is left—"

"Dad," Phil says, "it's not Grandpa." He's on the couch, reading *Audubon* magazine. "I didn't know you'd be so superstitious."

"Put it where I don't have to look at it," Shirley says, coming in from the kitchen. "I didn't want this, anyway. I didn't want him cremated."

"You shouldn't have had it done, then, Ma," Jeremy says.

"It was Daddy's wish. I had to follow it."

And Rachel is still standing there with the box in her hands, holding her grandfather, his bones and ashes. "Someone make up their mind, please," she says softly. "You don't want it in the kitchen, Ma. Daddy doesn't want it in his study. You don't want it in the bedroom. Or the living room. Where?"

It's MB who settles it. "We can just put the box in the closet for now." She takes it from Rachel and walks into the hall.

FORTY-TWO

Before the day is over, there is first a cable from Shirley's brother, Leonard, in London. Then, about ten P.M., a phone call. After he talks to her mother, Leonard speaks to Rachel.

"Rachel, this is your Uncle Leonard."

"I know. Hello, Uncle Leonard."

"Hello, dear, how are you?" He has an actor's voice, full, rich, deep. "Your mother's sent me pictures of you. I think you're a wonderful reincarnation of my mother."

"Grandma Eva?"

"Absolutely. The eyes, the mouth, everything. I put your picture in a frame next to a picture of my mother. Everyone comments on it. The resemblance is striking."

"Really?" No one has ever told her this. Not her mother, not her father. Izzy never said it.

"And now it's wonderful to hear your voice."

"Are you calling from London?"

"No, I'm at my country place. We were here when we got the news. So that's why I called. My father . . . well, your grandfather." A deep sigh crosses the ocean from England to the United States. "I hope someday you'll come to England and meet this part of your family. Your cousins will give you a wonderful welcome. You know, a family has to stay together. I have good reason to say that. Now I know it's too late, but just like I told your dear mother—she's a wonderful woman, I hope you know that—I regret bitterly, bitterly, that my father and I didn't make up our quarrel years ago."

"Uncle Leonard—"

"Yes, darling?"

"I spent a lot of time with Grandpa before he died." She has some vague notion of telling him something comforting about Izzy.

"Ah, you did? He was a difficult man, my father. Did you find him difficult?"

"Yes, especially at first." What if Leonard asks her what Izzy said about him? What will she say? The truth is, nothing, he never said anything about his son, only tightened his lips disdainfully when Leonard's name was brought up. "I—I didn't know him very well before that," she says quickly. "So I don't know too much about"—she hesitates—"about things. Family stuff."

"No, you wouldn't, of course, it was years ago. Years ago," he repeats. "So stupid." Then there's a silence, and in a moment he coughs and says, "Well, darling . . ." His voice trails off. "Yes, but it's the same thing, always the same thing. . . . You know, the time goes. I always thought there would be time. . . ." And then he asks to speak to Phil and Jeremy.

In the morning over breakfast, Jeremy says, "I almost forgot about that old quarrel Grandpa had with Uncle Leonard. It was a million years ago, wasn't it, Ma?"

"Well, when Leonard was a boy."

"I don't know why Uncle Leonard didn't want to talk to me," MB says. "I'm his great-niece."

"It was an expensive phone call, darling," Manny

233

says. He picks up the platter of pancakes and passes it across the table.

"I know, Grandpa, but I'm family, too."

"I don't even know Uncle Leonard," Jeremy said, "and he started talking pretty intimately to me, telling me about Grandpa being a real hard-nosed guy to deal with."

"He said the same thing to me," Rachel says.

"Did he say it that way? Hard-nosed?" Shirley asks.

Jeremy shakes his head. "Uh-uh. No, no, no way. He's got that actor's voice, he's got that actor's way of putting things. Mellifluous, you know? He said the same thing to you?" he asks Rachel. She nods. "I guess it was on his mind, so he said it. Maybe he's Grandpa's son, after all. Izzy always said what was on his mind, didn't he? Except, usually, it was something you might not want to hear."

"Jeremy, don't rake up the past." Shirley touches her younger son's arm.

"Ma, the way I feel now, I didn't always like it when I was on the receiving end from Grandpa. He twisted the knife plenty of times, but what the hell, the guy was honest. He wasn't bulling me. He meant what he said, and he wasn't getting anything out of it. How many people are there left in the world like that?"

"He was one of a kind," Manny says. "Very old-fashioned, straight as a die."

Phil starts laughing. "You know, I never had much trouble with Grandpa, except once when I was six years old and I had this loose tooth. Grandpa got tired of seeing me fiddling that tooth around." He looks at MB. "Did I ever tell you this, honey? Did you ever hear this story?"

"No, Dad."

"Well, you know how kids are. I'm wriggling that tooth back and forth, I want to get it out, so Grandpa Izzy says, 'Come here, I'll get that out for you.' He ties a string around the tooth, he takes the other end and knots it around a doorknob. I'm opening my mouth to say 'What are you doing, Grandpa,' but I never get the words out. He kicks open the door. That tooth went flying out of my mouth."

Everyone is laughing, a little horrified, too.

"Yeah," Phil says, "I'll never forget Grandpa saying to me, 'Now, that's modern dentistry.'"

"I remember once he had a hundred and three temperature," Manny says, "and the man went to work. It turned out he had pneumonia, he was staggering, but he put in his day's work. He was strong as a horse in his prime."

And then Shirley relates how when she was a little girl, Izzy took her to work with him once when her mother was sick. "He put me in a wheelbarrow, that's what I remember, sitting in that wheelbarrow and eating my lunch."

Only Rachel and MB haven't told a story about Izzy. Phil asks MB to speak. "I don't know what to say, Dad." She jiggles the bracelets on her arm. "Well, I was lucky to have a great-grandfather. I can say that. Most of the kids I know just have grandparents. Even though I didn't see Great-Grandfather very much, and even though, like I told Rachel, I hardly knew him, it was special."

"What about you, Rache?" Phil says. "You should say something."

"No, that's all right."

"No, go ahead . . . go ahead." A clamor of voices. Everyone looking at her. Waiting.

Suddenly, the image of herself walking down that

road in the rain comes back to Rachel, flashes up as if on a screen. She feels confused. "I ... I ... loved Grandpa." They look as if they are waiting for more. She shakes her head. "That's all I want to say."

They all go to the cemetery, squeezed into Manny's car, and scatter Izzy's ashes over Eva's grave. Shirley is crying again. It's a struggle for Rachel to hold back the tears. She really doesn't want to cry in front of everybody, or maybe she means in front of Jeremy, who stands there, somber but dry-eyed.

When they leave, there's a brief discussion about keeping Eva's stone cleared, and then Jeremy suggests planting a tree in Izzy's memory. "He liked the blue spruce on the corner near where he lived," Rachel says. And it's settled. They'll plant a blue spruce.

FORTY-THREE

"You want to go for a walk?" Jeremy says to Rachel. It's late in the afternoon. They have just said good-bye to Phil and MB, and Manny and Shirley are driving them to the airport.

"Let me get my jacket," Rachel says. It will be the first time she and Jeremy are alone together. It's a fair, lovely day. The air smells of apples. They walk around the neighborhood so Jeremy can check out the places he used to hang out when he was in high school. "My favorite corner," he says at the foot of Woodson Hill, and as they pass the QVR Drugstore, "Do you realize this used to be a scummy little supermarket where everyone got their sodas and chocolate-chip cookies?"

They circle around the high school, walk across the playing field, and end by going across the street and up the hill and toward Maplewood Cemetery. "That's where we used to go to smoke—whatever. The bad old days. You don't smoke, do you?" She shakes her head. "Good. Don't."

The hills and houses have a rosy, bricky color. The cemetery is quiet. They walk along the paths, then turn up a wooded hill.

"Jeremy, should I stop writing to you?"

"Why?"

Rachel shrugs. "You know . . . you hardly ever

answer. Maybe my letters are a nuisance to you."

"You don't mean that."

"No, I do. Sometimes I feel—well, what am I doing? I'm just writing into the void. Does he even read them?"

"Yes, he does. And he doesn't write letters to anyone."

"Okay, but how many people flood him with ten-page letters?"

He links his arm with hers. "I have to admit, not many. Listen, I like your letters. I like them a lot. I look forward to them."

"I hope you're not just saying that to make me feel good."

"Oh, Raaa-chel. Are you fishing?"

"If I am, I'm not catching much."

Jeremy squeezes her arm a little closer to him. "So what do you think? What are you going to do with your life now? Ma says you've been really wrapped up in Grandpa. I think she's kinda worried about you, kid."

"She's a worrier," Rachel says, as if she, herself, isn't. "She worries a lot about you, too."

"Yeah, I suppose."

Rachel sits down on a stone. It's warm from the sun, although the air is cool. Jeremy lies down on the ground and closes his eyes. He's got a stalk of dried grass in the corner of his mouth. "I guess I'm still not sure about the old man." He opens one eye and looks at Rachel.

"You mean Grandpa?"

"Uh-huh."

"Not sure how?"

"Oh . . . how I feel about him. You know, the real stuff. I said some stuff at home to make Ma feel better. I didn't want her to think I was holding a grudge." He laughs briefly. "But I guess I am. It's ridiculous. He's in his grave and I'm still stewing over what he said to me two years ago: 'You've lost your chance for a decent life!' How'd you like that dropped on you?"

He puts his arm over his eyes. "I should have settled it with him some way before he died. Should've come up here and visited him and told him what I thought, got it off my chest. That's what my girlfriend wanted me to do. And I didn't. And now I'm like Uncle Leonard. Time has run out for me and Grandpa."

Rachel's tired, a little dazed. There have been so many tears, so much talk, so many emotions. She draws up her knees. Her head goes down, she closes her eyes.

"So what do you think?" Jeremy says.

"I guess . . . I think . . . mostly that it's sad." She wants to say something else, something comforting. She wants to make Jeremy feel better, but sitting there, chewing on a piece of grass herself now, watching this brother of hers who she, mysteriously, cares for so much, watching him roll over onto his stomach and poke around in the dirt near an anthill, she realizes there is nothing she can say. The war between Izzy and Jeremy and, in fact, all the feelings Izzy aroused in his family, feelings that billowed over them like a wind-filled canopy while he lived, now can't simply be knocked down, rolled up, packed away, and forgotten because he's dead.

"There were so many years when I didn't know Grandpa at all," she says. "I guess I didn't like him much—or maybe I was a little scared of him."

"It was the same with all of us. It wasn't just you. He could be a pretty hard guy."

"Well, I know, that's what you said this morning.

Anyway, I'm glad that I finally—" she begins, and then she can't say it. Can't say she's glad she finally got to know him. The sky is clear and cloudless, the trees are blazing purely with autumn color, but she is all at once in a storm. Hard rain again, this time with thunder and lightning. This time, not grief but anger. Anger at Izzy, hard strikes of anger splitting the blue sky she's created out of their feeling for each other, anger for all those years he let slip by when they could have been knowing each other, when she could have loved him so much.

"What's the matter?" Jeremy says, leaning up on his elbows.

She's breathing fast. "I don't know, I just got so mad at Grandpa. I just—I don't know. I just— just—" She jumps up, walks around, sits down on the stone again, pounds her fists on her knees. "I'm angry! I'm mad. I'm so furious at him. God! I'm so mad!" She's screaming. Her eyes fill. "And I shouldn't be crying! I'm not going to cry! Why should I cry? I'm *mad* at him. That selfish, selfish, *selfish*—"

Jeremy scrubs his hand across her knee. Then he's getting up and sitting down on the stone next to her again, and he puts his arm around her shoulder and his cheek against her cheek. "Don't do this to yourself, Rachey. Take it easy. I'm sorry, I think I got you going, I shouldn't have said that about Izzy—"

"No! You can say anything you want. I'm not a kid, you're not influencing me!" Her nose is stuffing up. "I'm mad on my own, Jeremy, don't take so much credit!" She starts pounding his knee. She's barely aware of what she's doing. "I'm mad because of all that time Grandpa didn't do anything toward me. He didn't care about me. If he cared about me, he would have done something. You know he would have. It's such a waste, such a goddamn waste, because once I got to know him, I really loved him."

"It's bad losing somebody you love. I know it is. For whatever it's worth, it happened to me, too, a friend of mine, somebody I was in the Army with."

"Is that why you've had a lot of trouble in your life?" She feels bad enough, right now, to think that Izzy's dying is going to do that to her, too—ruin her life.

"No, stupid, it was the war that messed me up. Losing my friend was bad, but that was just part of it. You know, if someone dies and you're leading a normal, ordinary life, it's natural. People get old and die. Hang on to that thought. I don't mean you don't feel horrible and sad, but it's a natural part of things. War is something else. . . . War is . . ." He stops. "I don't want to get going on that."

Rachel bends over. "I'm sorry for you, Jeremy, but I'm sorrier for myself right now. I really loved him, Jeremy." And then she's crying again, really crying, harder than she has since Izzy died.

Jeremy sits with her, his arm around her, while she cries.

When she's done, he says, "You have a choice, buddy. You can wipe your face on this crummy-looking tissue or you can wipe it on my shirt."

"Shirt," she says, and rubs her face against his arm.

When they get up to walk home, she feels cleansed, light, maybe like a ray of light, something shining and clear. "I feel better," she says.

Jeremy nods. "Don't be surprised, though, if it happens again. It's like a seesaw, you know? You'll be okay for a while, maybe even for a long time,

241

standing right there in the middle, and then all of a sudden, *whoom,* just when you don't expect it, you'll go sliding down and hit hard."

"I'll let you know," she says.

"Yeah, you can write me about it."

"Maybe."

"What do you mean, maybe?"

"What I said." Their arms are linked, she feels terribly close to him, and she doesn't know why she's talking this way, as if she might not write him again. But then she thinks, *No, maybe I won't. Why should I, it's so unequal.* "Jeremy, as long as I'm writing to you and you're not giving anything back—"

"Record keeping?" he says. "Balancing the books?"

She lifts her shoulders. "I don't know. Maybe."

"Rachel. Your letters—they're important to me. I know I'm flippant a lot, but I don't just read your letters and toss them away."

She waits for him to say he'll write her, too, now and then, at least do better than a postcard every three years, but he doesn't say it and they go inside.

FORTY-FOUR

"I guess, really thinking about it, I always assumed when you missed someone, it was tangible," Rachel says, "something real you could grab and hold on to, but it's a not-there feeling. The absence of . . ."

"Of what?" Lewis says.

She takes her time answering, meanwhile checks out his lunch bag. They're outside school, sitting on the stone wall. "The absence, I guess, of whatever you're missing. For me, my grandfather. It's not some *thing,* it's like space, an emptiness."

Life has picked right up where Rachel left it off—school, writing, Helena, Lewis—but for days, she has felt as if she's acting a part, going through the motions she knows she ought to make but without belief. Her mind is like a dutiful little dog nudging her along: she's in school, she's going into the newspaper office in the basement, she's avoiding gym and writing English assignments. But where her heart continually tells her she ought to be is with Izzy.

Why aren't they out walking today? It's cold, but the sun is shining. At night, in dreams, she's in the hospital, cranking up Izzy's bed, filling his water pitcher. She dreams they are playing Scrabble. He's losing, and his gray, wild eyebrows jump up on his forehead in fury. "I'm a-winning," she says. "I'm finally a-winning a game from you, Old Grandpa-pa-pa!" And she wakes up laughing.

Another time, she has an elaborate, detailed dream about her and Alice Farnum carrying Izzy up a set of steps. At the top of the steps, he jumps off their joined hands. "Gotcha!" he says. "Got a free ride from you two girlies."

An odd thing happens. Coming home from work, she sees an old man heading for the bus. He's nothing like her grandfather, who had been large and big-boned with strong hands. This old man is small, there's a hump on his back, he's wearing a short black jacket and dusty, black shoes. The old man shuffles forward. He looks as if he's going to fall, and she takes his arm.

He glances at her in surprise, some alarm. Embarrassed, she releases him and he goes up the metal steps. She stands there anxiously, hoping for something, she doesn't know what. The old man's face appears at a window. Just as the bus is pulling away, he gives her a tiny wave.

Her heart fills in some strange and surprising way, and all the way home, against all logic, she feels that she has somehow helped her grandfather. And it all comes back to her. The walks, the games, the food, the coughing, Alice, the white dog, maple-walnut ice cream—everything. And the missing becomes very real, very tangible, a little clawed insect stuck in her chest.

Gradually, though, over the next weeks and through the winter, the thought of him slips to the side of her mind. For days at a time, she forgets. And she notices that other people, too, even her mother, talk less about Izzy. "We don't talk about Grandpa anymore," she says to her father.

"Oh, we do," he says. "Yes, we do, Rachey. But,

after all," he adds, "what do you expect? He's dead. He's gone."

Every now and then, she thinks about that handprint her grandfather left: "Five fingers and my initials, I.S." She tries to write a story about it. "The problem was," she writes, "there was more than one bridge he'd worked on and he couldn't remember which bridge was the right one. So though they searched, they never found the print, and he was then too weak to continue the search. He became sicker. He went into the hospital. And he died."

After that, she doesn't understand if the story is to go on or if it's finished. She thinks of showing it to Mr. Esparza, but the idea is frightening and she puts the story away in her desk.

In March, on a drizzly, warm, dirty-looking day, she goes back to West Creek Street. She doesn't do much more than walk up and down the street, counting bridges, but when she goes home, she calls Lewis and says, "Would you like to help me with something?"

"Sure."

"You say yes without even knowing what I'm going to ask."

"I draw the line at jumping off a bridge."

"It's funny that you say *bridge*. That's what it's about."

On Saturday, they spend the afternoon looking for the handprint, retracing the same walk she took with Izzy. Then the following week, they are there a couple of other afternoons. They are careful in their search, walking all the way around each bridge, getting down on their hands and knees and clearing away the debris.

Walking back, Lewis says, "You know, we're just

about done. . . . Do you think your grandfather's memory was okay?"

"It was perfect!"

"You're mad."

"I'm not mad."

"You're mad."

"I'm not mad," she says furiously. "I'm frustrated."

"Does it mean that much to you?"

"Obviously, Lewis. Obviously!"

"I'm not trying to be obnoxious, but why are you so upset?"

"I don't know why—I just want to find it so much and I got upset when you said we wouldn't find it. Maybe his memory wasn't so good. It could have been another bridge. Where would that be? Anywhere in the city . . . Well, I guess I should just let it go. Anyway, not waste more of your time."

"What do you mean, you'll keep looking on your own?"

"Yes."

"I'll keep looking with you."

"No, it's not fair of me to drag you along."

"I'm being selfish, Rachel. I know it means something special to you. I'd like to be with you if you find it."

So they keep looking, but still they don't find the handprint. It's Lewis's suggestion that they start all over again. "Maybe we missed something."

"I suppose."

"Definitely. We could have."

They begin again, but at the last bridge this time, working their way back to where they had originally started. This time, they're digging a little around the base of each bridge, scratching out the dirt. On Saturday, they decide to spend the entire day in a final,

246

all-out effort. They pack food into their knapsacks and meet early in the morning. The day has turned wintery, snowy, a wind is blowing, they are both wearing scarves and warm jackets. They search all morning, break for lunch, and go back again.

By late afternoon, they are on one of the last bridges. "After this, two more," Lewis says.

She feels a sudden dread. She isn't going to find it. There is no handprint. Her grandfather's memory was faulty. He was an old man, a sick old man. Kneeling, automatically scooping away the dirt, Rachel is close to tears.

"Nothing over here," Lewis calls from the other side. "You got anything? Hi," he says, coming sideways down the embankment.

"Nothing." But she continues clearing away the debris at the bottom of the wall. She's digging below the dirt line. Her fingers move automatically, her eyes scan the cleared places. She's not hoping, not the way she did when she first began; she's not expecting anything anymore. Just going through the motions. This bridge, then two more, then that's it.

"Do you realize the valuable experience we've gotten here, Rachel? We could hire out as bridge cleaners. I think the field would be ours."

She nods, answers automatically. "No competition." The first hollow she feels under her fingers doesn't register. Or the second. But then there are two more hollows. Four of them.

She pulls off her glove slowly, not believing, not daring to believe, scrapes away the last bit of dirt with her bare hand, and there it is. Another smaller hollow. Five hollows. Five fingers. And below it, I.S. Izzy's initials.

"Lewis." She points to the handprint. On the street above her, cars pass, one after the other. She places her hand flat against the wall, fitting her fingers into the outline of her grandfather's hand.

"I don't believe it," Lewis says. "We did it, we really did it." Then he's kneeling down and hugging her and saying, "Hey, we gotta celebrate."

She can't match Lewis's exuberance. Strange. She thought she would be wildly happy. She says quietly, "Yes, we did it." And she draws back, looking at her grandfather's handprint. Izzy did that. Just as he told her, years and years ago he put his hand in wet cement. Here is the proof. Here the handprint, here the initials. Nothing can remove them.

They are here now, she thinks, and they will still be here years from now, when she, herself, is old. And then, though today the whole sky is covered by gray clouds, for a moment she feels the sun on her head, as warm as a living hand.

FORTY-FIVE

"Lewis." Rachel catches up with him outside the gym. They walk through the hall together. Near the trophy case, they have to part. He's going upstairs. "See you later?" he says.

"Okay."

He walks away backward, smiling at her.

Suddenly, she runs up to him. "Thanks, Lewis."

"For what?"

"The bridge. For helping me. Sticking with me."

"Oh." He looks embarrassed. "You don't have to thank me, Rachel."

"Yes, I do. Thank you, Lewis."

"I didn't do anything."

"Yes, you did. You hung in there with me. Thank you."

"You said it already."

"I want to say it again. Thanks, Lewis."

"That makes about twelve times."

"Is that enough?"

"You can thank me some more."

"And let you get a swelled head?"

"Bye, Rachel, see you later."

"Bye, Lewis, see you later."

Norma Fox Mazer grew up in Glens Falls, New York, in the foothills of the Adirondack Mountains. She has been writing all her life and is the author of many highly acclaimed books for young readers, including *Taking Terri Mueller* (winner of the 1981 Edgar award for Best Juvenile Mystery); *A Figure of Speech* (a National Book Award nominee); *Saturday, the Twelfth of October* (Lewis Carroll Shelf Award); *Dear Bill, Remember Me?* (a *New York Times* Outstanding Book of the Year, an ALA Notable Book of the Year and Best Book for Young Adults); as well as *Downtown, Up in Seth's Room,* and *The Solid Gold Kid* (coauthored with her husband, novelist Harry Mazer), all of which were ALA Best Books for Young Adults. Ms. Mazer and her husband currently make their home in the Pompey Hills of central New York State.